GONE FOR YOU

BY
JAYNE FROST

SIXTH STREET PRESS
LAS VEGAS

COVER DESIGNED BY ALLY BISHOP

EDITIED BY ALLY BISHOP

PROOFREAD BY AUDREY MADDOX

WANT MORE SIXTH STREET BAND ROMANCES?

SIGN UP FOR MY MONTHLY NEWSLETTER AND GET THE LATEST, PLUS EARLY ACCESS TO NEW BOOKS AND SPECIAL, MEMBERS-ONLY ROMANCES!

TO GET STARTED, CLICK HERE:

WWW.JAYNEFROST.COM

To Jeff, the hero in all my stories.
My happily ever after. I love you always.

CHAPTER 1

My knee bounced up and down nervously as the cab inched along in the heavy afternoon traffic on I35. Pulling out my cell phone, I hit redial.

"Yeah?" Logan answered, sounding as frazzled as I felt.

"Have you heard anything?" Biting off a piece of my nail, I spit it on the floorboard.

From the front seat, the cab driver glared at me in the rearview mirror. I gave him an apologetic smile.

"Not in the last five minutes," Logan said, his exasperation evident. "I told you I'd call if I heard anything. Where are you?"

Looking around, I tried to find anything that looked remotely familiar. I was from Austin, for Christ's sake. The only time I ever ventured the two hundred miles north to Dallas was for a gig or a football game.

"Fuck, dude. I have no clue."

"Just get here as fast as you can. Christian's phone is still off."

The exasperation in Logan's voice had an edge of fear. The same fear I felt fluttering in my belly.

"I'll be there as soon as I can." I raked a hand through my hair. "Just call if…"

"Yeah, yeah, I will. Fuck. Lindsey just walked in. I gotta go."

Before I could reply, the line went dead. I was a buffer between Logan and our half-witted manager, Lindsey. The insensitive bitch could work him up in a hot minute under the best of circumstances. I met the driver's gaze in the mirror.

"Hey, man, how much farther?"

The cabbie gave me a half shrug. "About twenty minutes in this traffic."

Taking off my sunglasses, I rubbed my tired eyes. When I got the call that Christian had been in an accident, I jumped in the first cab I could find, not bothering to wait for the car service the label had on standby. At the moment, I regretted that particular decision. The fucking cab looked like it hadn't been cleaned in a year, and the driver looked like he hadn't bathed in just as long. His funk permeated the entire space.

Reaching over, I hit the button to crack the window. Nothing. I hit it again.

"Hey, man, can you open the window back here?" I barked over the music.

"No can do. Too many fumes out there."

I stared at him incredulously. Unfuckingbelievable. It smelled like a dog's ass in here, and the dude was oblivious. Dropping my head against the back of the seat, I closed my eyes.

"Before we get back to our super set, we've got some news," the DJ on the local rock station began in a somber voice. "I've just gotten word that Christian Sears, bassist for the band Caged, has been involved in an accident this afternoon in Dallas…"

"Oh, man. That's terrible," his female counterpart cut in. "I hope it's nothing serious."

Sitting bolt upright, I leaned forward. "Turn that up!"

Startled, the driver reached for the volume button on the radio. The speakers crackled to life.

"We haven't got any official word yet on his condition. Caged is scheduled to perform this Saturday at the AT&T Stadium. We'll keep y'all advised. Our thoughts are with you Christian." And just like that, the DJ went back into his cheery radio persona. "And now back to our Monday super set. Here's the

2

latest from Caged, 'Above Me,' on 97.1 The Eagle."

I hit the cracked, vinyl seat with a balled fist.

"I knew you looked familiar," the cabbie said, his smile fading when he met my gaze in the rearview mirror. "You're Colin, right? The guitarist from Caged?"

"Cameron," I said wearily. "Cameron Knight." I managed to give him a halfhearted smile.

"Man, I love your music." Cutting across two lanes of traffic, he jerked the cab onto the shoulder, spitting up gravel. "I'll get you there as soon as I can. Hold on."

My chest contracted as the air left my lungs, my shoulders sagging in relief. "Thanks, man, I appreciate it."

As the cab barreled past the four lanes of gridlock, I curled my fingers into the edge of the seat so I wouldn't slide around. The lump of dread in my throat was like coal—dry and bitter. I swallowed hard to dislodge it. And I prayed.

Scanning the waiting room of the emergency ward at Parkland Memorial, I spotted Logan seated in the corner, wearing dark sunglasses and a baseball cap pulled low on his head. He was doing his best to look inconspicuous. As inconspicuous as a six foot four inch rock star with long, blond hair in a three hundred dollar, custom fitted shirt could look. Lindsey was at his side, tapping on her iPhone.

"Cameron—" she started when I walked up.

Cutting her off, I looked at Logan. "Anything?"

"They're taking him back for a CAT scan or an MRI," he said quietly, looking around cautiously at the people that had begun to stare in our direction. "Something like that. They're checking for internal injuries. I haven't seen him yet. The doc says it doesn't look serious."

"Thank God." Pulling a plastic chair from against the wall, I sank onto it with a thud. "Where's Sean?" Looking around for the only member of our band that wasn't present, I noticed a couple of camera phones pointed in our direction.

"Cafeteria," Logan groused. "He left as soon as he heard Christian was in the clear. Fucker is a bottomless pit."

Chuckling, I took a couple deep breaths, the tension dissipating from my shoulders. "So now we just wait, huh?" Stretching my legs out in front of me, I crossed them at the ankle, dropping my gaze to the floor. I didn't want this little powwow to end up on TMZ or some crap tabloid show. Caged wasn't newsworthy enough to garner the attention of the mainstream press, but our celebrity made us ripe for tabloid fodder. Or at the very least, a clip on someone's blog. Annoying as shit, but it came with the territory.

"You guys should get out of here," Lindsey said, in her best authoritative voice.

She shrank in her seat when Logan and I swiveled our heads and scowled at her. The woman was not only a bad manager, she was fucking clueless. I wouldn't leave here without a court order, and even then, I'd rather go to jail.

Shaking his head, Logan looked from me to Lindsey.

"You know what, Lindsey? Why don't *you* get the fuck out of here?" he snapped, leveling her with a look of disdain. "And do…whatever it is that you do."

Bristling, she looked down at her phone when it began to ring. "I should take this."

Standing stiffly, she walked toward the automatic door.

"She needs to get out of my fucking sight before I strangle her." Logan watched her retreating back, his jaw clenched. "Her phone has been going off every five minutes since she walked in. Do you know she actually had the nerve to ask if I could do a phone interview while we waited?"

He continued to stare at Lindsey through the dirty windows. She was puffing on a cigarette, her arms flapping as she spoke. I was with Logan. I couldn't stand the bitch. Hiring a company from L.A. to manage us was the biggest mistake we ever made.

"Excuse me." The petite nurse stepped in front of us, a pink flush staining her cheeks. She was cute. Flaming red hair and green eyes as wide as saucers. She swept her gaze over my long

4

hair, her eyebrow cocking when she reached the tattoos winding down my arms, then gave Logan the same treatment. It was clear that she recognized us.

Normally, either Logan or I would be putting on the charm, vying shamelessly for her attention. Probably both of us.

"Um…Christian…Mr. Sears has been admitted for observation. He's going to be fine. He's asking for you," she stammered, flushing a deeper shade of crimson. "Both of you. He's asking for both of you."

We were on our feet, headed for the door before she finished.

"No, wait—you can't go through there." She closed the distance, regaining her composure. "You have to take the elevator. He's in room 402."

"Thanks, darlin'." I stopped in front of her, and she inhaled sharply. Brushing past me, Logan powered toward the bank of elevators. "Our friend Sean went to the cafeteria. He's about six foot one and—"

"I know what Sean looks like," she said shyly. "I'll tell the duty nurse to send him up as soon as he comes back."

"Thanks again…" Looking at the lanyard hanging in front of her perfect tits, I swept my eyes to hers. "Sophia."

"You're welcome…Cameron." Her smile turned from shy to seductive.

I glanced at her left hand. No wedding ring.

"Cameron!" Logan bellowed behind me. "Come on!"

Winking, I turned and sauntered toward him, stepping into the elevator.

"You're a fucking dog," he muttered, hitting the button for the fourth floor.

"Woof," I growled, the elevator doors whooshing closed on Sophia and her pretty green eyes still watching me from across the room.

"Dude, it's not funny." Christian winced, clutching his side. "My ribs are killing me."

Sitting at the foot of the bed, I shook my head. "That's what you fucking get. Why would you go for a bike ride in the middle of the city when you don't even know where you're going?"

We usually stayed in Irving, close to the old AT&T Stadium. We knew that area. But this time they booked us at the Omni Hotel in the middle of downtown Dallas. No bike lanes, and nothing but four lane highways and busy side streets as far as the eye could see.

"I needed the exercise." He shrugged sheepishly.

That proved my theory that the cure was worse than the disease. Of the four of us, only Christian would have a bike delivered so he could get in his ten miles instead of going to the gym at the hotel like a normal person.

"When are they letting you out of here?" Logan said seriously.

"Tomorrow." Christian stifled a yawn, his eyes drifting closed for a second as he spoke. "They're keeping me here in case I have an aneurysm or something."

The frown lines etched on Logan's face deepened.

Christian had suffered a slight concussion and bruised ribs. Other than the pain meds that were making him drowsy, he didn't appear any worse for the wear. The door swung open, and Sean Hudson, our drummer and the only member of our tight little foursome unaccounted for, stepped inside.

"Took you long enough, dickhead," Christian said, a drowsy smile creeping over his face. "I could have been dying while you were wolfing down a burrito."

Ignoring the comment, Sean crossed the room, laying a hand on Christian's shoulder. "You ever pull something like this again; I'll kick your ass. You'll be playing that bass from a wheelchair."

Christian smiled up at Sean, patting the hand that was pressed to his shoulder.

"I'm good, bro. Just a few bumps and bruises."

"Jesus," Logan groaned. "I need to get the fuck out of here. Before I grow a vagina."

"Don't…shit…don't make me laugh," Christian snorted, clutching his side. His shoulders quaked as he tried to suppress a laugh.

Our heads turned to the door when Lindsey's high-pitched squeal drifted into the room.

"I'm Mr. Sears's manager," she huffed. "Of course, he wants to see me."

Lindsey swept into the room with a nurse on her tail, her five inch heels clicking on the linoleum.

"Christian," she cooed in a saccharine sweet voice. "I'm so glad you're ok."

Christian nodded at the nurse, who looked at Lindsey like she wanted to snatch our manager's Chanel purse and strangle her with the gold chain. Giving Lindsey's back a withering glare, the nurse retreated from the room, her ponytail swinging behind her.

"Spreading sunshine wherever you go, eh, Lindsey?" Christian asked wearily, throwing an arm over his forehead.

Her mere presence and fake show of concern cast a pallor over the room. Dismissing Christian's comment, she looked at her watch.

"I hate to break this up." Lindsey reverted to her usual emotionless tone. "But I need all of you back at the hotel for a radio interview. Christian needs his rest. There's a limo waiting outside."

"Don't even start, Lindsey," Logan spat. "I'm not doing a fucking interview. Issue a statement or whatever. I'm not going to talk about the show, or the single, or anything else."

Rising to his feet, Logan pushed Sean out of the way, leaning over to say something in Christian's ear. I followed suit, grabbing Christian's hand and squeezing it.

"Let me know if you need anything." I cleared my throat to hide the emotion. "Get some rest."

Christian smiled, his unfocused eyes at half-mast.

Sliding his sunglasses on, Logan stepped around Lindsey and headed for the door. Sean followed, turning to smile at Christian before he stepped into the hallway. Surveying Lindsey in her monochromatic suit, with the flat smile frozen on her lips, I shook my head.

"Damn, Lindsey, do you have anything resembling a heart in there?" I matched her cold stare. "If I were you, I wouldn't push it."

She rolled her eyes, her heels clicking against the linoleum when she followed me out the door.

CHAPTER 2

"What the fuck is this?" I looked out the tinted window of the limo at the crowd of people, mostly female, milling around the parking lot of the Omni Hotel. They spilled out of the lobby, holding makeshift signs with "I LOVE YOU, CHRISTIAN" and "GET WELL, CHRIS" scrawled on them.

I didn't appreciate the intrusion, but their hearts were in the right place. Taking out my cell, I snapped a couple pictures and sent them to Christian. The warm feeling faded when a group of screaming girls descended on the limo. A smug look crossed Lindsey's face. This was no surprise. To her, at least.

"How did they know where we were staying?"

Lindsey's smile disintegrated under the weight of my stare.

"Aren't *you* supposed to keep shit like this from happening?" Glancing out the window, I tensed when several faces pressed against the glass.

"Yeah," Logan cut in. "isn't that what we pay you for, to keep us safe and anonymous between shows?"

"If you wanted to remain anonymous, maybe you should've stayed in Austin." Lifting her chin, Lindsey crossed her arms over her chest. "There's no such thing as bad publicity, boys."

Leaning forward, I clasped my hands in a death grip to keep

from choking her. "And if Christian were in a fucking coma, would that be 'bad publicity'? Or would you arrange a competition to find a new bass player? Maybe have it televised?"

The sparkle in her eyes told me I wasn't too far off the mark.

"Of course not." She picked an imaginary piece of lint off her skirt. "Christian's fine. I just thought since you missed the interview, we'd bring the interview to you."

Logan stared at her incredulously while Sean just shook his head, looking out the window. A van was parked in front of the entrance with "97.1 The Eagle" emblazoned on the side.

"Come on, boys." Lindsey plastered a smile on her face, sliding her sunglasses onto the bridge of her nose. "Your adoring fans are waiting. I've arranged for security to meet us."

"Security?" Logan roared. "Did you arrange for that before or after we found out that Christian was in the clear?" His blue eyes bore into hers, hidden behind her huge glasses. "Never mind, I already know."

"It doesn't matter, Logan," she said in a patronizing tone. "You're scheduled to do the interview, so *do* the interview. It will probably be broadcast all over the state with this crowd."

She looked out the window appreciatively, scooting closer to the door.

"Fuck this," Logan muttered, reclining against the seat. "I'm not going to be trapped in a room at this hotel all week because you wanted extra publicity." He turned to me. "Any ideas, Cam?"

Shrugging, I pulled out my phone, glancing at each of my bandmates.

"Make the call," Logan grumbled.

Hitting the button, I held the phone to my ear, waiting for my brother to answer. He picked up on the second ring.

"Hey, Chase." I pinched the bridge of my nose. "No, Christian's fine, but we have a little problem."

My brother was a miracle worker. He came through, just like always. It didn't take him ten minutes to firm up the arrangements. As the limo sped down the freeway, I sipped my beer, watching the landscape turn rural. Well, rural was a stretch, but at least skyscrapers weren't dotting the skyline any longer. After kicking Lindsey out at the Omni to deal with her mess, our group had relaxed.

"So what's the deal with this place?" Logan asked, looking absently at his phone.

"I dunno," I sighed. "Chase said it's the shit. He knows the manager. It's got great food and a spa. All the amenities."

I trusted Chase more than anyone else in the world. He was more than a brother to me. He was a mentor, a surrogate father, and the financial backer for the band from its inception. Before we even wrote our first song, Chase let us play at his club in Austin. He owned The Parish Bar, the largest venue on Sixth Street. Without him, Caged wouldn't have gotten any traction.

My phone vibrated next to me on the seat. Picking it up, I opened the text from Chase.

Your contact at the property is Lily Tennison. Get some rest. I booked three bungalows. There's another bungalow on hold for Chris when he gets out. Don't tell that bitch where you are.

Chuckling, I tapped a response.

Thanks, bro. No worries, Lindsey doesn't have a clue where we're headed. She's going to be blowing up your phone.

Seconds later, he returned: *She'll be lucky if I don't blow her ass all the way back to L.A. Call me later.*

Tucking my phone in my pocket, I took the last swallow from my Shiner Bock and tossed the bottle in the trash. The limo turned at the sign marked "Rosewood Mansion on Turtle Creek." Red bud trees dotted the long driveway, their pink petals scattered on the concrete.

Logan looked up when we pulled to a stop and stretched his arms over his head.

"I hope the staff at this place is as accommodating as the Omni." He gave me a wolfish grin.

We had only been at the Omni Hotel for two nights, but

Logan already managed to bang one of the bartenders. From the look of the cute little maid that I spotted leaving his room this morning, she delivered more than fresh towels.

"And you call me a dog?" I slid across the seat to wait for the driver to open the door. "Don't shit where you eat, Logan. Chase will kick your ass if his buddy tells him you defiled half the female staff."

"Whatever." Logan ran a hand through his long, blond hair. "I need something to occupy my time."

Logan's sexual escapades landed us in the press more than our music. The dude had an endless supply of energy when it came to entertaining the more willing of our fan base.

I was no slouch, but tonight I was worn out. If he were on the prowl, he'd be doing it without me. The only thing I needed was a good meal and a soft bed. Since this place didn't look like it specialized in happy endings, I'd wait until we ventured down to Harry Hines Boulevard, where the good old-fashioned massage parlors were. The girls there might not be licensed, but then what licensed therapist would let you bend them over the table when you were finished?

Squinting from the sudden brightness, I placed a foot on the pavement when the limo door swung open. I took in a lungful of the fragrant flowers from the trees that surrounded the circular driveway. After a string of nondescript hotels in cities I couldn't even remember, it was nice to be someplace that actually had some character.

My gaze fell on the figure that exited through the wooden doors a few yards away. Her blond hair swung from side to side, mimicking the sway of her hips. A smile played across her lips, crinkling the corners of her piercing blue eyes. My heart nearly stopped.

"Dude, close your mouth." Sean knocked shoulders with me when he stepped to my side.

Giving him a sidelong glance, I saw Logan smiling appreciatively at the girl, looking her up and down. *No way.* Stepping away from them, I nearly knocked her over in my attempt to reach her before she got caught in Logan's crosshairs.

Startled, she looked up at me, tucking a wisp of hair behind her ear. Fuck me, the girl was hot. Taking off my sunglasses, I gave her the most seductive grin I could muster.

Nothing.

"Mr. Noble?" She glanced down at the paperwork in her hand without acknowledging my lame attempt at flirtation.

"Knight, actually." I was hoping for a glimmer of recognition.

Her brows knit together, causing an adorable little crease to form on her forehead.

I *was* Cameron Noble. At least that's what my birth certificate said. But I dropped that shit as soon as Caged had a single on the charts, changing my name to Knight. My old man, Tyler Noble, the drunk that chased fame his whole life, was not going to get a nod of acknowledgement from me for anything I achieved.

"But you can call me Noble." Not to be deterred by her cool demeanor, I quirked a brow and leaned in. "Or anything else you want, as long as you say it with a smile."

Laughing nervously, she stuck out her hand. "I'm Lily Tennison. I'll be your personal events coordinator while you're here."

Taking her hand, I squeezed it gently. "I like the sound of that."

She took a step back, slipping her hand free. "Your brother explained the situation. If you would follow me to my office, I'd be happy to go over a list of the amenities and services we offer here at The Mansion. I'll also take care of any special requests you might have." Looking over my shoulder at Logan and Sean, she gave them a cheery smile. "Gentlemen, welcome to The Mansion."

Turning, she walked briskly toward the building, ignoring the snickers that erupted from our group.

"Special requests?" Logan chuckled, lowering his tone to nearly a whisper. "I've got her special request—*right here.*" He grabbed his crotch, waggling his brows at me.

Slapping him on the back of the head, I followed her into the lobby, putting some distance between me and the two asshats I was with. The guys couldn't hold it together for one fucking minute without acting like horny teenagers.

My cock stirred when the slit up the back of Lily's pencil skirt opened as she walked, showing a nice expanse of her silky thighs. Scowling, I looked down at my boots. Logan and Sean might have been acting like horny teenagers, but I was the one sporting a hard-on. Perfect.

The lobby was decorated with huge vases of freshly cut flowers and cushy, leather chairs with side tables made of rich, dark wood. Following Lily past the polished marble front desk, I noticed a number of guests staring in our direction.

"Over here we have our lounge and our steakhouse." Lily looked over her shoulder, giving a nod in the direction of the dimly lit space. "They are open for dinner only. Per your brother's request, I've secured a chef to take care of your meals, en suite. However, you can order anything off the menu and have it delivered, if you prefer."

Nodding, I kept my eyes trained on her face, hoping my cock would go into hibernation. Lily's tongue darted out, sweeping her lip when she looked down at her paperwork. A perfect, pink tongue. Caressing the softest, pinkest lips I'd ever seen in my life.

She disappeared ahead of us, turning down a hallway where the executive offices were housed. I took the opportunity to stick my hand in my pocket and adjust my erection.

"You got a problem there, son?" Logan clapped my shoulder as he strode past me.

"Mind your own damn business," I muttered, moving to his side. "And stop with the fucking sex jokes."

Logan gave me a sidelong glance, peering at me over his sunglasses. "Dude, I'm not the one with the semi."

Rolling my eyes, I stepped through the door of Lily's large office. A leather sofa was pushed against the wall. Three winged chairs with rich upholstery sat in front of the large cherry desk. Oil paintings and other artwork hung on every wall. I wandered over to a group of four charcoal sketches next to the window. A large "L" with a small flower dotted the right hand corner of each one. The gritty cityscapes didn't match the rest of the office's motif.

"These are really nice." I nodded appreciatively, leaning in closer to examine the details before turning to her.

"Um, t-thanks," she stammered. The crease in her brow grew more pronounced when she noticed me looking at her. She dropped her eyes to the paperwork on her desk. I grinned, ambling over to take a seat in the winged chair in front of the desk.

"I've taken the liberty of contacting a personal shopper at Neiman Marcus." She lifted her gaze, taking in our tattered jeans and t-shirts. "If you could provide me with your sizes, I'll have some things brought over for you until you can retrieve your luggage from the Omni."

"Is there something wrong with the way we're dressed?" Logan removed his sunglasses, leaning forward and propping his elbows on his knees.

"Absolutely not." She shifted in her seat. "I assumed since you didn't have any clean clothes, you might want to order a few things. It's totally up to you. There's no dress code on the property, with the exception of the hotel dining area."

Clasping her hands on top of the paperwork on her desk, she gave us a sincere smile. "Look, y'all, I'm here to help. I'm sorry to hear about your friend." Her gaze fell on mine, holding it for a second. "Is he alright, if you don't mind me asking?"

"Fine," I said, studying the blue depths of her irises. "Just a little banged up."

She nodded sympathetically. "Let me get this paperwork out of the way. I'm sure you've had a trying day."

Turning to the computer on the side table, she punched in the information from the sheet of paper on her desk. A few minutes later she stood, handing each of us a fat envelope.

"It was nice to meet y'all." She extended a hand to Logan, and then to Sean. "Please let me know if I can be of any assistance during your stay. The bungalows are out back, at the far end of the property. Would you like me to call for a cart to take you there?"

"I'm sure we'll manage," Logan said with a chuckle, giving

her a wide grin. "Thanks for all your help."

He nodded at Sean, who thanked Lily as well before following Logan out of the office. She stepped around the desk and clasped her hands in front of her. I waited until the guys were out of earshot and closed the distance between us.

"So what do you do for fun around here?"

That perfect, pink tongue darted out again. I assumed she wasn't aware of what she was doing, but I couldn't tear my gaze from her lips. An arc of electricity flowed between us, drawing me to her like a magnet.

"Um…" She trailed off, seeming unsure of her words. "I've enclosed this brochure in the envelope I gave you. We have—"

"I mean, what do *you* do for fun, Lily?" Placing a hand on her arm, the hair on the back of my neck stood on end. Definitely electricity.

Staring at me for a moment, her arm dropped limply to her side. "I work." She smiled up at me. "And I go to school. I don't have much time for fun."

With that, she stepped toward the door, holding it open. Nodding, I shoved the envelope in my back pocket, leaning toward her on my way out. She smelled just like the freshly cut flowers in the lobby. Like a spring day.

"That's a shame, Lily. Everyone could use a little fun."

It took a shitload of self-control not to look back when I sauntered down the hallway.

Before I made it five steps, the door clicked shut behind me.

CHAPTER 3

The grounds at The Mansion were as elegant as the interior. A huge pool with an outdoor bar sat empty, the tables and chairs covered. Steam was rising from a hot tub the size of a small swimming pool, although none of the guests were brave enough to make use of it in February.

Passing through the gate to the private bungalows, I pulled the envelope from my pocket and searched for the suite number. I trekked across the tree-lined path until I stumbled across the right one, tucked behind a small grouping of trees.

Inserting my key in the lock, I stepped inside, dropping my sunglasses on the marble sofa table. The room was top notch, sporting a gourmet kitchen, a bar, and a huge master suite. A baby grand piano sat in the corner in front of a picture window that overlooked the grounds.

Strolling into the kitchen, I pulled open the refrigerator. It was stocked with all the necessities: bottled water, a twelve pack of Shiner Bock, and a tray filled with cheese and fruit.

I grabbed a bottle of water and pulled out the tray, tearing off the plastic wrap as I walked to the sitting area. The ringing phone echoed in the cavernous space. I looked around, spotting it on the Louis XIV desk in the corner.

Shit.

Ignoring the persistent ring, I stretched out on the sofa and munched on a piece of cheese. I cursed under my breath. If I was going to go to the gym and burn off the tension that had my back twisted in knots, I would need some workout gear.

Popping a strawberry into my mouth, I pulled the envelope from my pocket. Lily's card fell out when I turned it upside down to remove the contents. A number was scrawled on the back in delicate script.

Taking out my cell phone, I punched in the number.

"Lily Tennison."

"Lily," I said as I opened the brochure, laying it across my lap. "This is Cameron."

No response.

"Cameron *Knight*." As I sat up, my feet hit the floor with a thud. I couldn't be that fucking forgettable. "I was just in your—"

"Of course, Mr. Knight. What can I do for you?"

I scowled. She couldn't see me, but I knew I was scowling. And that was enough. Time to teach Ms. Tennison a little lesson. She wouldn't be forgetting me after I got through with her.

"I need you to fetch me some workout clothes, darlin'. Size large."

What the fuck? I looked down at the blank screen on my phone. Standing, I hit redial. The phone rang twice and went to voicemail. And then it sank in. She hung up on me. *Me.*

Sinking back onto the sofa, I placed the phone on the table and stared at it. The last woman that hung up on me was my mama. And that was years ago.

I chewed another strawberry, deliberating. The cell phone sat idle. Mocking me.

Jerking my head at the pounding on the door, I stood and walked cautiously across the room. Through the peephole, the only thing visible was the top of a woman's head. And a mass of blond hair. I stepped back when the door shook from another loud rap.

"Can I help you?" I ventured, without making a move to unlock the door.

"Mr. Knight, this is Lily Tenn—"

Swinging the door open before she finished, I leaned against the frame, giving her a half smile.

"Hey, Lily," I drawled, hitching a brow. "I believe we were disconnected. You didn't have to come all the way out here to find out my size."

"I-I didn't," she bit out through clenched teeth. "I don't fetch, Mr. Knight."

"Just an expression." I folded my arms across my chest. "No need to get all worked up."

"I'm not worked up. I-I just…"

She was too fucking cute, stammering and turning red. Kicking the door open, I turned and walked back across the room. I picked up a fork and speared a piece of melon, turning to her in the doorway.

"Are you going to come in?" I sank onto the couch, putting my feet on the expensive as fuck coffee table. "I thought of a few more things while you were on your way over."

Lily's shoulders sagged in resignation. Stepping inside the door, she clasped her hands in front of her.

"My email address is on the card," she said quietly. "If you send me an email, I'll make sure to pass it on to our personal shopper."

"Now, why would I do that?" Leaning forward, I speared another piece of melon. "You're already here."

Realizing her little show of defiance had backfired, she squared her shoulders and closed the door, walking purposefully toward the desk. I cocked my head, taking in another eyeful of her luscious backside when she passed. This time I didn't bother to hide my appreciation when she turned, a notebook and pen in her hand.

She took a calming breath. "What exactly can I get for you, Mr. Knight?"

Holding the pen so tightly I could see the white in her knuckles, she waited for me to tick off my list.

"The workout clothes I mentioned. Size large. A couple pairs of jeans. Boot cut. Size 32x36. T-shirts and socks." Draping an arm over the back of the couch, I looked her up and down. "And underwear."

Scribbling furiously, she didn't look up. "Boxers, briefs…" Her pen finally came to rest, and a smile hitched up one side of her lips. "…*or panties?*"

I choked on the piece of melon trying to make its way down my throat. Coughing and sputtering, I leaned forward. Lily casually walked to the table, handing me the half empty bottle of water.

Grabbing it from her, I took a large swallow. A couple of tears sprang to my eyes as I looked up at her. The girl was way too cocky for her own good. Clearing my throat, I took another swig, finishing the bottle.

"Well?" She looked at me innocently.

"Boxers," I growled.

Ripping the paper from the notepad, she folded the note and dropped the pad on the table.

"I'll make sure to have these delivered as soon as possible." Stepping over my legs, her skirt hiked up her thighs as she went to leave.

Resisting the urge to pull her down on the sectional, I fell back against the cushions and watched her stalk out of the room, slamming the door soundly behind her.

I muted the TV when I heard a rap on the door. Lily. I sauntered to the door, my shoulders slumping when I peered through the peephole and saw a balding man in his mid-forties.

"Can I help you?" I asked cautiously.

"Mr. Knight? I'm Dave, your valet." Straightening, he lifted the nametag on the front of his white smock. "I've brought your dinner, along with some items Ms. Tennison asked me to deliver."

Standing back from the door, I flipped the deadbolt and

pulled it open. Dave's grin widened. "May I come in, sir?"

"Of course." I opened the door wider when I saw the cart. "And call me Cameron."

"Very well, sir." He backed into the room, pulling the cart over the threshold. "Where would you like to eat, sir?"

Running a hand through my hair, I pointed at the table in front of the TV. No matter how hard I tried, I would never get used to a man many years older calling me "sir" just because he happened to be serving my dinner. Or washing my car. My father was a horse's ass, but my mama taught me to respect my elders.

Dave placed the cart next to the table and began to unload plates. Grabbing a couple, I set them down next to the others. He smiled at me appreciatively.

"May I turn down your bed—"

Cutting him off, I patted him on the back. "If you call me 'sir' one more time, I'm going to send you packing." Sitting on the couch, I looked up at him. "I'm grown, Dave; I think I can manage to pull back the comforter all by myself."

"Very well..." Dave was on the verge of another "sir" when I leveled him with a warning glare. Clearing his throat, he stood awkwardly. "If you don't mind, I'll check the refrigerator and see what needs to be replenished. I'll be right back to take your order for breakfast, assuming you will be dining in your room."

I pointed at the two empty water bottles. "That's all I've taken from the fridge, plus some fruit and cheese, and I noticed an extra case of water in the pantry. So no worries." Intercepting the ever efficient valet when he tried to remove the silver covers from the plates of food, I motioned for him to sit. He looked at me, eyes wide. "Take a load off, Dave. I insist."

Positioning himself on the edge of the chair, he folded his hands in his lap. I pushed a plate of buffalo wings in his direction. Having ordered a sample of most of the appetizers on the menu, I had way too much food in front of me.

"I really should be getting back," he said, his eyes falling on the heaping plates of food.

From the looks of him, Dave liked his groceries.

"Aren't you supposed to be my personal go-to guy or something?" Licking the sauce from my fingers, I raised a brow at him.

"Yes, sir…Cameron…sir."

"Well, then go to it, son." I nudged the plate a little closer to him. "Let's not let this food go to waste."

Picking up an appetizer plate, he served himself a single buffalo wing. I shook my head.

"You can do better than that." I lifted my chin toward the rest of the feast.

Dave loaded his plate with potato skins, cheese sticks, and a few other tidbits. Truth be told, the band was on the end of a two month tour. While I should savor eating alone, I just wasn't that kind of guy. I preferred to dine with my band mates, the roadies, just about anybody.

Biting into a potato skin, I shifted my gaze to Dave. "So how long have you worked at The Mansion?"

Swallowing the remainder of a cheese stick, his eyes drifted to the ceiling. "Let's see. Twenty-five years." He nodded to himself in confirmation. "I started here the year my daughter Sylvia was born."

He chuckled, looking down at his plate.

"What's so funny?" I reached for my water.

"My daughter…not Sylvia…Raquel, she would keel over if she knew I was eating dinner with Cameron Knight."

I paused with the water bottle halfway to my mouth. "You know who I am?"

Dave nodded. "I have two daughters, Mr.…Cameron." He chuckled. "I'm a little long in the tooth, but I'm not completely out of touch."

I barked out a laugh. "Two daughters, huh? Bet that keeps you on your toes."

"You have no idea."

Being on the road, I had a *very* good idea. But I wanted to have a quiet dinner, not give Dave a heart attack. Sitting back, I noticed the Neiman Marcus bags hanging from the handle of the cart.

"Are those the packages Lily sent over?" I asked, intrigued.

"Yes, sir."

Dave tried to get up, but I motioned for him to finish, standing to retrieve the bags myself. After walking to the couch with the four overfilled bags, I upended the first one. An array of pastel pink and lavender t-shirts tumbled out. Shaking my head, I pulled the jeans from the next bag. The first pair was super skinny, with jewel embellished pockets. The next pair was boot cut, but the jewels that encrusted the pockets somehow managed to wind their way all the way down the outer seam. Cringing, I was afraid to look in the next bag. When I pulled out a handful of silk boxers that looked like Cupid had thrown up all over them, I laughed out loud.

Turning to Dave, I noticed he'd clamped his lips together to keep from laughing.

I walked to the kitchen, grabbing two bottles of Shiner and a couple bottles of water. I offered him one of each. Hesitating, he reached for the Shiner.

Plopping on the couch, I twisted the cap off my beer before turning to Dave.

"So, tell me, Dave," I lifted a brow, "How well do you know Lily Tennison?

CHAPTER 4

"Come in." Lily looked up when I stepped into her office, her jaw dropping to her desk when she saw me.

"I just wanted to stop by and thank you for the new duds you had delivered last night." Shoving my hands in the pockets of the black skinny jeans, I sauntered over to her desk and leaned in. "I would sit down, but these jeans are so fucking tight, I might lose the ability to procreate."

Blinking, she tried to stifle a giggle. "I-I think they look g-great." She was unable to hold back a snort of laughter from escaping.

"Really? Is it the pink t-shirt?" Stepping back, I turned to give her a view of the rhinestones that covered the pockets. "Or the jewels on my ass that make it work?"

Leaning back in her chair, she let loose, a husky laugh erupting from deep in her chest. "It's the whole thing." She moved her hand in front of her in a circular motion. "It all works."

Stepping around her desk, I grabbed the arms of her chair, startling a yip out of her.

"Very funny, Lily." I leaned in until our faces were a few inches apart. I could smell her shampoo. The cinnamon on her breath. The perfume that clung to her. "You're lucky I can pull off any look. A lesser man wouldn't be comfortable in pink."

Releasing the arms of the chair, I walked around to the front of the desk and sat on the edge of the chair. "As much as I'd like to continue discussing my fabulous wardrobe, I'm actually here to book a package."

Lily tucked a wisp of hair behind her ear and sat up straighter in her chair. "Of course." She pulled out a laminated copy of the brochure. "What package are you interested in, or would you like to create your own?"

"The Essence of Texas," I said casually.

"Um...The Essence of Texas?" Swallowing hard, she looked down at the brochure. "Of course. Cameron—Mr. Knight—are you aware of the…" She sighed, looking me dead in the eye. "It's very expensive."

"I understand it's a two day package." Cocking my head, I smiled. "And the cost is in the neighborhood of ten thousand dollars. That doesn't sound too steep. Is there something about the package that you don't recommend?"

"No!" She was quick to shake her head. "It's a wonderful package. A private tour of the Dallas Museum and the Nasher Sculpting Center." She pulled open a drawer and produced several other brochures, laying them in front of me. "The artwork is really beautiful. Aside from that, you get to choose a night at the ballet or the opera." Her fingers brushed the photos of the art from the museum.

Our eyes locked when she looked up, her smile fading when I covered her hand with mine.

Clearing her throat, she pulled her hand away and grabbed a Post-it from the dispenser.

"What dates were you interested in?"

"Thursday and Friday." Leaning back in the chair, I let my gaze drift over her face while she chewed her lip, studying the calendar in front of her.

"That might be tough, considering it's such short notice. I'll have to call the venues and get back with you." The same adorable crease popped out on her forehead.

"No worries." I rose to my feet and headed for the door. "I'm sure you'll get it handled, darlin'."

"Wait!"

I glanced over my shoulder. "Yes?"

"Would you prefer the opera or the ballet?"

Shrugging, I smiled. "I'm not sure. What do you recommend?"

Her face broke into a huge grin. "The ballet is wonderful."

"The ballet it is."

"I talked to Chase this morning." I reached past Logan and grabbed the pot of coffee. "Here's a list of interviews that we're obligated to do to fulfill the contract." Handing him a copy, I poured the liquid gold into my cup.

"Hmmm," he grunted, pulling his sunglasses down a little to peruse the list.

Our table was in the back of the dining area, as far away from the other guests as we could get. After talking to Lily, I had slipped back to my room to change into yesterday's clothes. I was prepared to play out her little joke in private, but I wasn't going to risk ending up in the tabloids wearing that getup.

"Dude." Logan looked over his glasses at me with red-rimmed eyes. "I'm not doing any interviews today. Besides," he pointed at the first interview on the list, "I'm sure you're more equipped to handle this interview than I am."

Nodding, I took a sip of coffee.

"Wendy Palmer, 102.1 The Edge" was at the top of the list. Usually it was an either/or proposition for most interviews. Either Logan or I could do them.

Not this one.

A million years ago when Caged was just a garage band, Wendy Palmer was a first year communications major at the University of Texas at Austin. She managed to finagle an assignment as the music critic for both the school newspaper and radio station. Quite a coup for a freshman. Soon she was doing interviews with large scale Texas bands that favored the Sixth Street live music scene. She made her bones, worked her way up the media ladder, by scoring interviews with the top Austin bands.

Wendy followed Caged to every dingy venue on Sixth Street. Or should I say, she followed me. When we got our big break, headlining at The Parish, Wendy was there. She helped me celebrate.

Naked.

Our relationship— if you could call it that—was mutually beneficial.

I never thought much about Wendy these days, unless Caged was making a pass through Dallas. Sometimes we ended up right back where we started. In bed. Although a bed wasn't a prerequisite. A dressing room, the tour bus, or even a bathroom had served its purpose throughout the years. The last few times I was passing through, it was strictly business. A thirty minute interview, and I was out the door. Her latest gig as afternoon DJ at 102.1 The Edge placed her firmly in one of the top ten markets in the country.

"Don't worry; I'll take care of Wendy." Glancing at Logan, I cringed when he waggled his eyebrows at me. "But I need you to do me a favor."

"What?" he groaned, rubbing his forehead.

Obviously, his night had been a bit more eventful than mine.

"I'm going to be off the grid Thursday and Friday," I said, hoping like shit he didn't ask too many questions. "Can you hold down the fort?"

Leaning back in his chair, he surveyed me. "Where you gonna be?"

Pushing the eggs around on my plate, I didn't make eye contact. "Just some personal shit I gotta take care of."

"What personal shit?"

The question hung in the air between us. Logan was like family. Even closer. But we were competitive. Women were an Olympic sport for us. If we got our sights set on the same woman, all bets were off. Fortunately, no woman had ever been important enough to come between us.

Lifting my eyes to meet his questioning gaze, my stomach roiled at the thought of him with Lily.

"Cameron Noble!" Turning my head to the guy walking toward our table, I raised a brow. "You look just like your brother. I'd recognize you anywhere." He reached for my hand. "I'm Greg, the manager here. I've known Chase for years."

"Nice to meet you, Greg." Smiling, I extended my hand.

He shook it and turned to Logan, who didn't look up from his plate. Shifting from foot to foot, Greg shoved his hands in his pockets. I guess he wanted more than a meet and greet.

"Pull up a chair." I motioned toward the other side of the table. "Join us."

Logan's foot found my shin under the table, though he didn't look up. Greg eagerly pulled up a chair.

"Nice place you have here." I pushed my plate of half-eaten food away.

"Thanks." Greg nodded at the server who dropped off a cup of coffee. "I'm glad y'all are enjoying yourself." Ignoring Logan's grunt, he added sugar and cream, stirring them in slowly. "I've got tickets to your show. Not the best seats, but..."

Time to pony up for the solid Greg did by providing the posh accommodations at a moment's notice. "How many tickets do you need?"

His face lit up. "Just two." Looking down at his cup of coffee, a coy smile hitched up one corner of his lips. "You know how it is. I'm trying to impress a girl with my connections."

"I would think that wouldn't be a problem," I said with a chuckle. "You've got a great events coordinator on site."

His smile widened. "Since the events coordinator is the girl I'm trying to impress, it would kind of ruin the surprise."

My stomach did a little flip. *No way.*

"Isn't that kind of taboo? Propositioning your employees?"

Well, shit. That had sounded better in my head. Greg either didn't notice, or he was too embarrassed about being caught with his hand in the cookie jar to protest.

"Technically, it's a little sketchy." He shrugged. "But Lily's already given her notice. She's graduating in May."

I nodded, choking down another sip of my coffee. Dave had told me all about Lily finishing her fine arts degree at Southern Methodist University. That's the reason I was dropping $10K on "The Essence of Texas" package.

Eyeing Greg, I tried to suppress a smirk. If the dude had his sights set on impressing Lily, he'd need to up his game. Bringing her to one of my concerts after I dropped a small fortune for a couple of dates wasn't likely to do the trick.

"Let me see what I can do about the tickets," I hedged. "We're not exactly on speaking terms with our manager right now, and she controls that shit."

It wasn't a lie, but it wasn't the truth, either. I could get Greg tickets to the show. Front row. But I wasn't down to watch him grinding on Lily while I serenaded them from the stage if our dates didn't turn out the way I planned. *Awkward.*

"Awesome." Greg extended his hand for another shake.

After looking at it for a second, I reached across the table and shook it.

Game on. Poor chump had no idea.

Something caught Greg's attention over my shoulder. He licked his lips, and I swear his pupils dilated. The click of high heels on polished travertine…it had to be Lily. I had the urge to piss on her leg just to mark my territory.

"Hey y'all," she said cheerily. "I think there was some mix-up with your personal shopping order yesterday, Cameron. I've placed another order, and it should be delivered this afternoon." Her gaze shifted to Logan. "Chloe will have the items you ordered delivered to your room as soon as they arrive, Mr. Cage."

Chloe?

"Thanks, Lily. Tell her to drop them by anytime." He traced the rim of his coffee cup with his index finger, a ghost of a smile on his lips.

I'm guessing Chloe might have had something to do with Logan's bedraggled appearance. The pink flush that crept into Lily's cheeks confirmed it.

"If any of the items don't fit, bag them up, and I'll have them returned." She kept her gaze fixed on his face, despite her glowing cheeks.

"I don't think that will be a problem." Logan winked. "Chloe knows my size."

Greg chuckled when Lily turned a deeper shade of pink. Logan's gaze drifted across the room to a willowy redhead that perused the fruit bar, adding items to her plate.

"Excuse me." Logan pushed his chair back and dropped his napkin on the table.

Sauntering across the room, he greeted the redhead, leaning forward to whisper in her ear. She placed a hand on his chest and giggled.

"Chloe?" I lifted a brow, looking to Lily and Greg for confirmation.

They nodded.

"So I'm guessing Chloe is Logan's personal valet?"

Lily's flush was nearing crimson on the color matrix.

"And—I'm making a wild guess here," I said with a grin, "that Sean has an equally fetching companion for the week."

"I told you before, Cameron, we don't fetch," Lily snapped, crossing her arms across her chest defensively. "But I'm sure Sean is quite satisfied with my choice."

Greg gave me a wolfish grin. "Which one of our lovely valets did Lily choose for you, Cameron?"

"Dave Salsida," I deadpanned, looking directly into Lily's sky blue eyes. "I'm not complaining, though. He might not be my type, but his knowledge of the property and the staff is enlightening."

"Of course," Greg said with a chuckle. "Dave is one of our best."

I hid my smile. Lily might be acting disinterested, but she was as clear as a pane of glass. If she truly didn't give a shit, I'm positive she would have chosen someone other than Dave to help stock my refrigerator and bring me my messages.

"I should be getting back." Greg rose from his chair. "Can I walk you to your office, Lily?"

"Sure," she mumbled, glancing at her phone.

"I just got the last confirmation for your package." Looking up, she gave me a self-satisfied smile. "The limo will pick y'all up at 9 a.m. Thursday. Dave will bring over your itinerary this afternoon."

Shaking my head, I stood. "No can do. I have a radio interview this afternoon."

"That's fine. He'll leave it on the desk in your bungalow." Lily slid her phone in her pocket. "Or slip it under the door, if you prefer."

"Nah, I'm not comfortable with that." I shook my head, dismissing her suggestion. "I want everything to be perfect. Why don't you drop by the bungalow Thursday morning to make sure it's all set?"

"Of course, Cameron." She glared at me.

Clueless, Greg took out his phone, frowning at the screen. "I've got to go see about something off property." He dropped a hand to Lily's back. "I'll see you tonight."

She continued to glare at me, seemingly unaware of the poor sap trying to get her attention.

"Lily?" he said.

"What?" Startled, she tore her gaze from mine and turned to him. "I'm sorry, you were saying?"

Narrowing his eyes, he dropped his hand from her back. "I've got a meeting off property. I'll see you tonight."

She nodded. "Of course."

"It was nice meeting you, Cameron." Greg clapped me on the back. "I'm sure I'll see you before you leave."

"Sure. Thanks," I said, my eyes on Lily the whole time.

Greg walked away, looking over his shoulder at us, with his phone pressed to his ear.

"What's going on tonight?" I asked dryly. "Hot date? Thought you didn't have time for fun?"

"I don't," she huffed. "It's just a work thing. There's a new pianist Greg's thinking about hiring for the lounge. He wants my opinion."

It sounded like a date to me. Or a way to get in her panties. Since I had a plan to get there first, I didn't appreciate Greg cock-blocking me. I was only here for a few days. He lived here. He could always…

Looking into Lily's sky blue eyes, I let the wretched thought die. Whatever happened when I was gone was none of my business. But Greg would have a hell of a time getting to first base while I was around.

I shrugged. "Have a good time." She clamped her mouth shut when I glided past her.

As I stalked to the front desk, the clerk turned to me, her eyes going wide. I rested my arms on the polished marble, smiling at her coyly.

"Can I help you, Mr. Knight?" Her tone was breathy.

Cute. She was really fucking cute. My gaze flickered down to the nametag pinned to her chest, admiring what was underneath. Not today, Olivia. But I'll remember you next time I'm passing through.

"You sure can, darlin'," I drawled. "What's the dress code in the lounge?"

"Business casual." She twirled a strand of her dark hair around her finger.

I didn't own anything business, and my casual was too casual for the lounge. I glanced over my shoulder when the hair on the back of my neck registered Lily's presence. She walked toward her office, looking down at her phone without acknowledging me. I could always ask her to contact the personal shopper, but I didn't want her to think I was desperate to hear her voice. Which I was.

"Then I guess you'd better tell me where the nearest mall is around these parts."

CHAPTER 5

W here are you going?" Logan pushed his way into the bungalow and went straight to the fridge, where he grabbed a bottle of beer. He wandered over to the sectional and turned on the TV, flipping to the pay per view.

"Dude, no porn," I muttered, holding up one of the ties I had picked up at Saks. "What are you doing in here anyway?"

He flipped through the stations, finally settling on ESPN. I knew the answer. He was trapped. We never spent more than two nights in the same city, and if we did, we usually changed hotels.

We were here until Saturday, *and so was Chloe*. Logan wasn't going to be a total dick, but he wasn't stupid. She might get the wrong idea if they spent the entire week enjoying each other's company.

"Just hanging out." He gave me a sidelong glance as I stood in front of the mirror, holding up each tie. "What are you getting all decked out for?" He narrowed his eyes suspiciously.

Ignoring his question, I draped a tie over each shoulder. "Red or grey?"

"Dude, do I look like Heidi Klum?"

Shaking my head, I walked to the bedroom to finish getting

dressed.

"Are you going to tell me where you're going?" he called after me.

Cringing, I pulled the pins out of the dress shirt. "I thought I'd go to the lounge."

Logan stood at the door, watching me fumble with the tie. "Who's the girl?"

I didn't look up. Whatever I said would come out wrong. If I told him I was stalking Lily for a sport fuck, he'd make it a competition. On the other hand, if I admitted I couldn't stop thinking about her, I'd never hear the end of it.

When I didn't answer, he stomped across the room and grabbed my shoulder, spinning me around.

"If you ever tell anyone I helped you tie your tie, I'll make sure the world knows you cried like a bitch the first time you rode the Texas Giant."

Slapping his hand away, I turned back to the mirror, glaring at him in the reflection. It was the biggest fucking roller coaster in the country, and I was twelve years old.

"I'm going to hang out here." Grabbing a magazine, he dropped on the bed. "What?" He looked up, quirking a brow. "If you have to go through this much trouble to turn this chick's head, she isn't going to fall into your bed, dude."

"You never know."

Ordering my second Jack and Coke, I stared straight ahead, my eyes fixed on the mirror behind the bar. I had the perfect vantage point to see anyone who walked through the door, without looking like I was waiting around. Pathetically. In a coat and tie.

I tugged at my collar.

A curvy brunette slid into the seat next to me, meeting my gaze in the mirror. Smiling coyly, she looked down at my drink when the bartender asked what she wanted.

"Whatever he's having," she said, turning to look at my profile.

The bartender smirked, turning to fix the drink while he glanced at us in the mirror. I'm sure he'd seen this ritual played out. Daily. Smiling, I tipped my glass to her before I took the next gulp of my drink.

Taking it as an invitation, she turned in her seat, crossing her legs to reveal the top of her thigh high stocking. It was kind of cliché. But I was intrigued. My tattoos were covered and my long hair was combed back in a respectable fashion. As respectable as I could manage, considering the length. Just an average guy, stopping in for a drink after work.

"I'm Tiffany." Handing her credit card to the bartender, she picked up the crystal rocks glass he placed in front of her.

"Cameron."

Stirring her drink, she looked at me over the rim of the glass. "So, Cameron," she said with a sigh. "Are you waiting for someone?"

Tiffany looked a little sad. Or bored. She set her drink on the coaster, surveying the room. Definitely bored. Like she'd done this a million times, and she was over it.

"Not really," I said truthfully, my gaze drifting to the door.

Seeing no other hot prospects, she turned her attention back to me, affixing a fake smile on her lips. "Are you from around here?"

"Austin. Just here for the week."

Her shoulders sagged a little, and her smile wilted. Music filled the lounge from the piano in the corner. Couples paired off, making their way to the dance floor.

A guy slid onto the barstool on the other side of Tiffany. Meeting my gaze over her shoulder, he lifted a brow. Shrugging, I turned away.

He proceeded to chat up Tiffany, offering to buy her next drink. The fake smile on her lips got wider, matching the fake laugh that rolled off her tongue.

Yeah, looks like Tiffany might be getting lucky tonight. Or not, considering the faint tan line on his ring finger.

I was about to order my third drink when they walked in. Greg glanced around the room, spying a table in the corner. Placing his hand on the small of Lily's back, he guided her there and motioned for the cocktail server when they sat down.

Lily looked around the room nervously, her eyes finding mine in the mirror. Her mouth fell open in surprise. Greg leaned in to speak to her, but she kept her gaze on my back, nodding at whatever he said.

The guy was kind of a douche. And way too smarmy for Lily. I took a gulp of the fresh drink the bartender set in front of me.

"That guy is really butchering the tunes over there," he muttered. "Don't suppose you know how to play any of this easy listening crap, huh, Cameron?" Smiling wryly, he dragged a rag across the bar. "You are Cameron Knight, right?"

"That's me." Pulling a fifty-dollar bill from my front pocket, I slid it across the polished marble, arching a brow at him. "But I'd appreciate it if you keep that info on the down low. I really don't feel like blowing my cover."

"Sure thing." He nodded, slipping the bill in his pocket. "Let me know if there's anything else I can get you."

The bartender made himself scarce, chatting with a few customers at the end of the bar.

After the fourth drink and several clandestine looks from Lily, who couldn't take her eyes off my back, I signed my tab and wobbled to my feet. This wasn't my scene. I didn't skulk around in dimly lit bars, trying to pick up chicks.

Pulling the tie loose from my collar, I glanced over at Lily. Greg was several inches closer, but her eyes were firmly trained on me. Turning, she gave him a thin smile before standing up and making her way across the room. She slipped into the alcove on the side of the bar.

Maybe it was the four drinks that clouded my judgment. Or those damn blue eyes that sought me out since the moment she walked in. But I followed her into the dimly lit hallway. Propping myself against the wall, I waited outside the ladies' room like a desperate stalker.

Lily's eyes went wide when the door swung open and she spotted me.

"Cameron." Tucking a stand of hair behind her ear, she stepped into the hallway. "What are you doing here?"

I pushed off the wall. "Waiting for you," I said simply. "Like you knew I would."

"I don't—I didn't—" she stammered.

"'Course you did, darlin'. You've been looking at me all night."

Red stains crept into her cheeks, and she turned toward the door. Barking a laugh, I grabbed her arm.

"So you're just going to leave me standing here?"

She froze in her spot. Waiting. Lily wasn't the type of girl to throw herself into my arms and follow me back to my room for a night of wild sex. Therefore, she wasn't my type. But something about her made her wrong in all the right ways—forbidden.

"How's your meeting going with Greg?"

"Awful," she sighed, her shoulders sagging. "Apparently, I'm the only one who didn't think this was a date. He keeps trying to touch me."

Fuck me. The girl was really naïve. Of course he was trying to touch her.

"He wants to do a lot more," I said with a chuckle.

She turned to me, her forehead creased in confusion.

"How do you know that?" Narrowing her eyes suspiciously, she cocked her head. "Did he say something about me?"

My laugh echoed off the walls in the small space.

"He didn't have to. You're beautiful, Lily." I stepped in front of her, tracing the curve of her jaw with my thumb. "And funny. And smart…"

Her blue eyes drifted shut when I leaned forward, brushing my lips against hers. She tasted like honey with a hint of bourbon. Sweet and hot. It was all over for me. The twinge in my chest turned to a tug. A pull. *A complication.*

Pulling away, I raked a hand through my hair. Lily smiled, warm and inviting. It was like the chicken inviting the fox into the henhouse.

"I've got an early wake-up call." My tone was low and husky. "I'll see you around, Lily."

I turned and pushed the door open, cutting my eyes to Greg. Lily stumbled out and crashed into my back.

"Sorry," she mumbled, smoothing her skirt before taking a step in his direction. I could almost see the drool on his chin from across the room.

No way.

Grabbing Lily's hand, I laced our fingers, pulling her into the lobby.

"I-I'm not going to your room with you, Cameron."

"I don't remember inviting you, darlin'." Leading her to the revolving door, I nudged her forward and followed her in. "I'm walking you to your car."

"You don't have to do that." Stepping out into the cool air, she picked up her pace. "Thanks, Cameron."

The tightness in my chest got stronger with each step she took. Shoving my hands in my pockets, I jogged to her side, stealing a glance out of the corner of my eye. She shook her head, but she didn't protest, and a faint smile curved her mouth. After we walked past several rows of cars, she stopped beside an ancient Honda.

"This is me." Shoving the key in the lock, she pulled open the door. "Thanks again."

"Drive safe."

Lily slid behind the wheel, and the car spluttered twice before rumbling to life. I raised a hand, and she waved hesitantly. Watching the taillights fade, I didn't move from my spot until she was out of sight.

CHAPTER 6

I went to bed thinking about Lily, and she was in my head in the morning. An ice cold shower didn't help. Two hours in the gym, running until I was ready to puke, barely took the edge off.

Now I was fatigued *and* horny. And late. Standing at the front desk, I raked a hand through my hair.

"So you're telling me there isn't a limo available—" I growled, my gaze drifting to her gold nametag, "—Brandy?"

"Mr. Knight," she squeaked, "I'm so sorry. I don't know what happened. Chloe booked our last limo for Mr. Cage." Flustered, she twisted her hands in front of her.

"Do you have an idea when they'll be back?" I tried to keep the edge out of my voice.

"Let me check." Reaching for the phone, her hand shook slightly as she punched in the number.

Shit. I wasn't my father. Acting like an asshole wasn't going to get me to the radio station any faster.

"No worries, darlin'." Resting my forearms on the desk, I leaned forward, giving her a disarming smile. "Can you call me a cab? I've got an appointment at a radio station in Addison."

Nodding, she held up a finger and turned her back to whisper into the phone.

Fuck. I looked at my watch and bit my lip. If I didn't get out of here soon, I'd have to reschedule the interview with Wendy.

Pulling out my phone, I slid my finger across the screen and hit Logan's number.

Music blared in the background when he picked up. "Yeah?"

"Where are you, Logan?" I snapped. "You took the last limo, and I've got that fucking interview with Wendy."

He laughed. "I'm on my way to the Omni to pick up my shit, and then Chloe is going to show me what passes for live music here in Big D."

Logan knew damn well what passed for live music here. Deep Ellum in downtown Dallas was home to a dozen live music hot spots. Caged had played at Trees, one of the larger venues, on more than one occasion

"Really, dude? Doesn't that chick know who you are?" I snorted. "You've probably played Deep Ellum more times than she's been there."

He kept up the farce. "It's supposed to be kickin'. You should head out there later."

"Maybe I *would*, if I had a *ride*." Giving up, I shook my head. "Just stay out of The Prophet, ok? Tracy's bouncer boyfriend is still looking to separate your head from your shoulders."

It had been almost a year since we played that gig, but the 250 pound gorilla bouncer was not likely to forget walking in on Logan and his bartender girlfriend half-naked in the dressing room.

"Loosen up, Cameron."

"I'm fine," I said with a snort. "Ain't no bounty on my head. Hey, pick up my stuff when you're at the Omni. I'm probably going to get a cab to the interview."

My mouth went dry when Lily rounded the corner, wearing a pair of ripped jeans and a sweater that barely covered her midriff. Her pink Converse sneakers squeaked on the stone floor as she walked toward me.

"I've gotta go." Hanging up on Logan, I slid the phone in my pocket.

"Where are you headed?" she said, pulling her sunglasses

out of her purse.

"A radio interview in Addison." I leaned against the granite pillar next to the front desk and looked her up and down. "I'm waiting on a cab."

Wisps of hair fell out of her loose bun, begging me to pull it down and run my hands through it.

"No need. I'll drive you." She glanced at her watch. "We better get out of here before traffic gets too heavy."

"Are you volunteering to be my chauffeur, darlin'?" I joked.

"Actually, I am." Turning on her heel, she glanced over her shoulder. "Are you coming?"

Peeling my boots from the floor, I followed her out of the lobby.

"Lily, stop." I grabbed her arm as she trotted toward the parking lot. "That's really not necessary."

I was already having serious doubts about the package I booked. My instinct was to offer it as a promotional giveaway at one of my interviews. The thought of wasting $10K made me want to hurl. But the vision of walking around a museum with my dick hard enough to cut diamonds was worse. I could already feel it stirring in my pants.

Lily sighed in frustration. "B-Brandy called me. It's my f-fault. It's the middle of the week, and I didn't have a car service on s-standby. T-two limos are usually sufficient, but Chloe b-booked one, and a group of businessmen took the other for a g-golf outing. I-I'm s-sorry..." Cringing, she seemed to fumble for the words until she finally gave up.

"Don't worry about it." My hand reached for a strand of hair that had tangled in her lip gloss.

"I'm fine taking a cab."

"No."

The effort it took for her to get that one word out left her so damned flustered, I got the urge to sweep her into my arms and give her a hug. A genuine hug—not the kind that led to ripping off her clothes. I stepped back a foot, shoving my hands in my pockets.

"P-please." She looked up at me. "L-let me do t-this. I'm

really s-sorry about the mix-up."

The more wound up she got, the more her speech fragment-ed. The tug in my chest only added to the urge to comfort her. It was…unexpected. Blowing out a breath, I slipped on my sun-glasses to hide my eyes.

"Sure thing. Lead the way."

She brightened immediately, breathing an audible sigh be-fore turning toward the parking lot.

"You've seen my car, right?" Looking at me out of the cor-ner of her eye, she gauged my reaction. "So you know it's a little r-rough."

"I can handle it."

"G-good." Moving ahead of me, she hustled to the driver's side of the Honda parked in the first space. It looked much worse in the light of day. "Let me unlock the door." Grinning, she jan-gled her keys. "No automatic locks."

Sliding behind the wheel, she reached over and pulled the knob on the passenger door. The door creaked loudly when I pulled it open. I climbed into the seat, and the door popped when I slammed it shut. The bucket of bolts didn't look like it would make it out of the parking lot, let alone across town.

"Not what you're used to, huh?" Lily raised her voice over the roar of the engine.

It was more than a roar. It was a cry for help. As in, *please put me the fuck out of my misery.*

"Not lately."

"No disparaging remarks about Bianca." She patted the dashboard. "She's old as dirt, but she's paid for, and she's reliable as shit."

"I don't suppose Bianca has a GPS." I quirked a brow at her.

"They didn't even have GPS technology when Bianca came off the line." Suppressing a laugh, she pulled her phone from her pocket and tossed it to me. "Press the map on the home screen; I've already loaded the address of the radio station."

After I opened the app, the automated voice of the navigator offered the voiceover of our route.

Lily bobbed her head to the radio playing quietly in the

background as we pulled out onto the freeway. When she started to sing, my attraction turned to near frenzy. I looked around for a distraction.

"What are those?" I pointed to the two large portfolios and several sketchpads in the backseat.

"N-nothing. Just some drawings."

Grabbing a sketchpad off the back floorboard, I opened it to the first page. A charcoal of a city street with dilapidated storefronts, slick with rain, was so lifelike it felt like you stepped into the picture.

"C-Cameron!" She nearly swerved into the median as she reached over to grab the sketchpad.

"Watch the road, darlin'." Turning sideways to avoid her reach, I flipped from page to page, each drawing better than the last.

"Fuck, Lily." I spotted the "L" in the corner with the little flower. "These are amazing."

The drawings in her office—they were hers. She glanced at the page with a shy smile, full of pride.

"Is this your medium of choice?"

She seemed surprised by the question.

"No, actually, I like oil." She sighed. "But I think my charcoals might show more promise, according to my teachers, at least." Staring straight ahead, her mouth turned down at the corners. "I always dreamed of being an artist," she said quietly.

Thumbing through the pages again, I studied the details. "You *are* an artist."

It was the truth. Each and every one of her drawings was gallery worthy. Closing the sketchpad, I laid it on the floorboard. The urge to rip off her clothes had my body thrumming. But the desire to kiss her was greater.

"Did you always know?" she asked.

"Know?"

"About the music. That you wanted to be a musician?"

This was the question that I was asked in most interviews. It may not have been worded in exactly that fashion, but the sentiment was the same. The explanation was slightly more complicated, and something I never detailed. There were very few people that knew the truth.

"Have you ever heard of the Noble Ones?" Looking out the side window to avoid her questioning gaze, I studied the glass buildings that jutted into the sky.

"They were a band in the '80s, right? I think I've heard their songs."

I laughed dryly. "Song. As in, *one song*."

The car inched forward in the afternoon traffic, the fumes from the diesels turning my stomach almost as much as the memories.

"That was my father's band. Music was his dream. His whole life." My lip curled inadvertently. "And booze. Sometimes women, as long as they weren't my mother."

My eyes drifted to hers. The adorable crease in her brow deepened as she alternated glances between the road and me.

"You can't choose your parents." Frowning slightly, her voice dropped to a whisper. "I should know."

We both looked down when the GPS dinged. Lily yelped and whipped her head around to check the traffic behind us. She punched the gas and jerked the car across two lanes of traffic. My heart jumped into my throat as she nearly clipped an SUV when she merged into the exit lane.

"Fuck, yeah!" She hit the dashboard, and her eyes twinkled with excitement. "Never doubt the mighty Bianca!"

"Damn, girl," I croaked, turning my head to make sure no one had a gun on us. "You know we're in Texas, right? You're going to get us killed."

Her throaty laughter took up the entire car, filling the space and creeping into my body. Like something I wanted to hear every day. My thoughts drifted into dangerous territory. Relationship territory. My lifestyle didn't allow for relationships, so I didn't do them. I didn't even try.

If there was one thing I learned from Tyler Noble, it was never make a promise you couldn't keep. The man was full of empty promises. Those promises led to two children and the awkward moment he left without a word. My mama used to say we were just like him, Chase and me. She didn't say it out of spite. She said it out of reverence. She never got over the bastard. Or their sorry-ass relationship.

The car jerked to a stop in front of the radio station, rousing me from my thoughts.

"We're here." Lily turned, giving me a brilliant smile.

My heart tugged at the sight of it.

Reaching over, I brushed the hair off her face.

"That we are, darlin'."

CHAPTER 7

The red light blinked off, signaling a commercial break. Pulling one of the headphones off my ear, I reached for the water bottle. The difficult part was over. Christian's accident kept most of the questions centered on his recovery, which I could handle. Lily sat in a chair outside the booth, watching the interview through the glass.

"How are you liking your stay here in Dallas?" Wendy gave me a sly grin. "Are you staying out of trouble?"

"I've been staying out of trouble. So far." Leaning back in my chair, I ignored the tugging in my chest that felt like a noose around my neck.

That was a damn lie. Lily was trouble with a capital 'T'. I wasn't staying out of trouble. I was chasing it.

"That's a shame," Wendy cooed. "There's no fun in that."

"I've still got a few days." I leaned forward, giving her a sexy smile. "You know I'm all about the trouble."

"Sixty seconds," the disjointed voice crackled through the speaker.

Shifting my gaze to Lily, her furrowed brow was the only thing that let me know our conversation carried outside the booth. Adjusting the headphones, I waited for the music to wind down, looking anywhere but at the wall of windows where Lily sat.

"We're back with Cameron Knight, guitarist for the band Caged," Wendy announced. "He's been staying here in Dallas while Christian Sears recovers from the traffic accident he was involved in earlier this week. So, Cameron, our listeners are dying to know. Are you seeing anyone special?"

Wendy had to throw that one in. It was obligatory. Taking the microphone, I let the answer roll off my tongue without hesitation.

"I'm very single at the moment, Wendy. What you see is what you get."

She laughed, husky and filled with innuendo. "At the moment? Does that mean the notorious Cameron Knight might be on the lookout for something a little more permanent?" Her eyes flickered to the phones that were lighting up like a Christmas tree. "I'm sure that more than a few of your female admirers might want to know where the line to fill that position forms."

I felt stripped to the bone. And scared shitless. "Don't go putting words in my mouth." My gaze drifted to Lily, locking on her like a heat-seeking missile. "But if the right girl came along… you never know."

Following my gaze, Wendy smiled. "Well, there you have it, ladies, straight from the horse's mouth. Cameron Knight is on the prowl." She laughed. "Maybe one of you can catch his eye while he's in town. Thanks, Cameron. We're looking forward to Caged Saturday night at AT&T Stadium in Arlington. It's Wicked Wendy at 102.1…The Eddddggge! We'll be right back."

Yanking off my earphones, I stood awkwardly. Suddenly, I felt more like Cameron Noble than Cameron Knight.

Wendy hit a couple of buttons before pulling one earphone off her ear.

"Thanks for coming in, Cam. It's always great to see you." Looking up at me, she winked. "I guess inviting you over to my place is out of the question?"

A nervous laugh bubbled from my chest. "Not this time, Wendy." Leaning forward, I brushed my lips against her cheek.

"Hope to see you at the show."

"Wouldn't miss it, baby."

Giving me an amused grin, she replaced her earphones. I grabbed my bottle of water and headed out of the booth, shaking hands with a couple of guys before I raised a brow at Lily.

"You ready to roll?"

It took a full fifteen minutes in heavy traffic before Lily said a word.

"So that's pretty much what you do all day." She chuckled. "Give interviews and flirt with disc jockeys?"

"I manage to fit in some music every once in a while." I laughed. "And trust me, that wasn't flirting. You'll know when I'm flirting."

"Wendy looked pretty flirty to me." Glancing at me out of the corner of her eye, she assessed me with a blank expression. "She was very interested in your dating situation."

Blowing out a breath, I pondered my response.

"Well, that's probably because I don't date," I said slowly. "I haven't dated anyone since high school."

Tilting her head back, she laughed uproariously. "Really? I don't see you spending many nights alone, Cameron."

Resting my arm on the console that separated us, I brushed my pinky against hers. She made no move to pull away.

"There's a big difference between a date and a random chick I hook up with on the road."

My honesty might send her running for the hills, but there was no use pretending. She wasn't a fool. When a couple minutes passed, and she didn't move her arm or throw me out of the car, I was calling it a win.

"How about you, Lily?"

She kept a straight face. "I've had a couple dates since high school."

"I figured that." I laughed. "Nothing serious though?"

I held my breath and waited for the answer, trying to act casual. It had been a while since I had to try this hard to get information from a chick.

"I don't have time." She sighed. "Between school and working two jobs, sleep is the only thing I do when I get a few extra hours. I don't even have time to paint anymore." She frowned at that.

"Two jobs? You don't make enough at The Mansion?"

"Not really. School is expensive, so I have to pick up bartending shifts to make ends meet."

We rode in silence until she pulled into the tree-lined driveway, jerking to a stop at the entrance of The Mansion.

"Sorry about the mix-up today." Turning to look at me, she flashed a quick smile. "I had fun, though."

Her eyes were soft and relaxed, and damned if I didn't want to drag her inside with me.

"Have dinner with me tonight," I said impulsively.

Her eyes clouded with hesitation. "I can't." She pulled her hand away. "I'm meeting a demanding client in the morning. He purchased a very expensive package. I need to be up bright and early to make sure everything is perfect for him."

She was right. It wasn't a good idea. But I was a selfish bastard, and I wanted her in my bed. Wanted it so bad I could taste it. I figured since Lily was not like the girls I hooked up with, taking her to the museum, the ballet, and all that shit would probably satisfy her three date requirement. It was the pregame warm-up. To be followed by a night of mind-blowing sex. And then I'd be gone.

Stick to the plan. Before I could stop myself, I leaned forward and placed a light kiss on her lips.

"It's just dinner, Lily." Lifting her chin with my finger, I kissed her again.

The ice blue of her eyes was melting into a clear, blue sky. Full of possibilities. She searched my face. I was asking for more than dinner.

"Ok," she relented, looking around nervously. "But not in

the dining room. Go to the bungalow, and I'll be right behind you. I work here, Cameron."

Nodding, I pushed the door open and wobbled to my feet. I didn't want to open my mouth and give her a reason to change her mind.

I headed for the lobby at a good clip, ignoring the band around my chest that was tightening by the minute.

CHAPTER 8

Inserting the key into the slot, I pushed open the bungalow door. Dave stood in the kitchen, preparing a tray of fruit and cheese.

SHIT.

"Cameron!" His smile fell away a little when he noticed my blank expression.

"Hi, Dave." Covering my shock with a smile, I walked toward the kitchen. "I didn't realize…" I rubbed the back of my neck, my mind racing for something to say. Fuck it. "Dave, I'm going to need some privacy. I've got someone coming by."

Recognition dawned, a smile crinkling the corners of his eyes. "Of course. Two minutes, and I'll be out of your hair."

Wiping his hands on his apron, he hastily assembled the tray and placed it in the fridge while I chewed my lip. I smiled reassuringly when his eyes met mine.

Jerking my head toward the light rap on the door, I froze. "Guess she's early," I said, arching a brow.

Sauntering to the door, I swung it open, looking down at Lily with my best attempt at surprise.

"Hey, Lily." Resting my hand high on the doorframe, I cocked my head, motioning at Dave with my eyes. "What are you doing here?"

The term "deer in headlights" aptly described her, frozen on the doorstep with her mouth slightly open.

"I-uh…" Her gaze shifted from me to Dave, her eyes getting wider as the seconds ticked by.

"Oh, that's right." Dropping my hand, I stepped aside for her to enter. "You were going to bring the itinerary for the tour. Let's make it quick. I'm expecting…someone."

She opened her mouth to speak, but a cute little squeak tumbled out. She cleared her throat.

"Yeah, I brought it. The itinerary. For the…thing." She stuttered over the words as she stepped into the room. "Hi, Dave." She waved, color washing over her porcelain skin.

Luckily, my back was to Dave when I cringed. Lily's was not when she mimicked the expression.

Nodding at her, he suppressed a smile while he hurried to finish up. Dave had been around too long and had seen too much for us to fool him with our little charade. He had the same expression as when I had pumped him for information about Lily. Amused. We stood awkwardly, staring at anything but each other while he finished.

"Mr. Knight, I'll be leaving now." Dave lumbered toward us with a tray of fruit rinds, wearing a jovial smile. I pulled the door open for him. "Nice to see you, Miss Tennison. When your guest arrives, Mr. Knight, ring the kitchen if you'd like to order dinner. Have a good night. Both of you."

Lily folded her arms over her chest, her gaze fixed on the door sliding shut. Flipping the deadbolt, I closed the distance between us.

"You think he suspects anything?" She looked up, the wrinkle on her forehead begging me to smooth it away.

"No, darlin'," I lied, pulling her against me. "Besides, we haven't done anything."

Yet.

Dropping my mouth to hers, I quieted her protest, threading my hands through her hair. I swallowed her soft moan, letting it echo in my chest. Lifting her off the ground, I buried my face in her neck. The tip of my tongue made a slow path across her collarbone. Her skin was sweet as honey.

"Fuck, Lily, you're sweet," I groaned. "So fucking sweet."

She hooked her leg around mine, and my cock stirred when our hips met. She pressed against me, a silent assent that stilled my heart. Before I had time to think, I swept her in my arms and carried her toward the bedroom.

She searched my face when I slid her down my body and onto the bed. Leaning over, I untied the laces of my boots, kicking them to the side. The sight of her had me in a near frenzy. I pulled the t-shirt over my head and unbuttoned my jeans. Giving her a smile, I pulled out my wallet and dug out a condom, throwing it on the bed. She snapped her head around, looking at the foil package then back to me.

Sliding my zipper down, I let my jeans fall to the floor and dropped to my knees in front of her.

"I think you've got too many clothes on, darlin'." I reached down to slip the Converse off her feet. "Let's see what we can do about that. Lay back for me."

I stilled when she hesitated, bringing her hand to my face. Her lips were parted, as if to ask me something.

"You okay?" I rose to eye level, leaning into her touch.

"Fine," she murmured, dragging my lips to hers for a slow kiss.

Breaking away, she lowered herself to the mattress, never taking her eyes off me. I stared at her, fingering the button of her jeans for a second before popping it open. Tugging at her zipper, I finally chanced a peek at the smooth skin of her stomach. I leaned forward and planted a soft kiss just below her belly button. And I was gone. Gone for her.

I pulled off her jeans with a couple of tugs, and her hand clamped down on mine when I reached for her panties. Slipping out of my grasp, she moved to the head of the bed.

"Come here." She reached out a hand for me, pulling me toward her when I grabbed it.

Positioning myself on top of her, I ground my cock into her thigh. My mouth came down hard on hers, tangling our tongues in a fury. I devoured her, my desire to get close, *closer*, driving me to distraction.

Breaking our connection abruptly, she brought her hand to my face. "What's your hurry, Cameron?"

The question hung between us as I stared down at her. "I..."

Before I could finish, she pulled me to her, pressing a soft kiss on my bottom lip. There was no frenzy. No promise of wild abandon. Just a lingering taste of honey, and her fingers in my hair. Sliding her tongue between my lips, she rolled it over mine in a gentle wave.

The tension that built behind the kiss sent pulses of electricity shooting through me. It was the sweetest kind of torture. The kind that you couldn't satisfy. Not in weeks. Or months.

Or two days.

I rolled on my back, the thought sobering me like a bucket of cold water. Lily froze beside me. Reaching down, I found her hand, lacing our fingers as the weight of it settled on me.

"I didn't want you to stop," she said quietly. "Just slow down."

"I'm not stopping, baby. Just catching my breath."

I bit my lip at the endearment and the sentiment behind it.

Rising to her knees beside me, she looked down on me with hesitation. It had been years since I'd seen anything resembling hesitation on a woman's face. Every woman I'd been with knew what she was getting. Or whom they were getting. Cameron Knight. For an hour, maybe longer. No expectations, no repeat performances. It was a song I knew as well as any I played on stage. But Lily stripped that away. It was Cameron Noble she saw.

Finding the hem of her shirt, she pulled it over her head. Pebbled nipples strained against the gauzy fabric of her lavender bra. She wasn't wearing fuck-me lingerie. Or even a push up bra. She hadn't cajoled her way backstage or onto my tour bus.

I was a selfish prick for playing this game, and even more selfish for what I was about to do.

Pulling her toward me, I kissed her softly. "You're beautiful, Lily," I murmured against her mouth. I wanted her to feel the words, the rush of breath when I said them. "Stay with me to-night."

My heart sank when she pulled away. Her leaving was the best thing. At least one of us had the self-control to realize it.

Standing, she looked over her shoulder at me. "Can you help me with this?" Turning her face to the wall, she gathered her hair to one side.

I moved to the side of the bed, pushing to my feet. "With what?"

My hands hovered above her shoulders before I gave in, resting them on her smooth skin.

"With my bra. It's a little tricky." After a few seconds, she turned to face me. "If you're going to make love to me, I'd prefer to have all my clothes off." While looking into my eyes, she slid her panties over her hips, letting them fall to the floor. "If you just want to fuck, I guess we can leave it on."

CHAPTER 9

Pulling her toward me, my hands were in her hair, tilting her head back so I could devour her mouth. She didn't hesitate, locking her arms around my neck and moaning when I scored my teeth along her bottom lip.

"Turn around, baby."

Dropping her arms to her sides, she kept her eyes closed, turning in my arms. I ran my hands up her taut stomach, skimming the underside of her breasts with my thumbs.

It was my decision. My choice. There was a part of me that wanted to bend her over and make her moan, with a clear understanding that this was as far as it would go. When the sun came up tomorrow or the next day, I'd be nothing but a memory.

For that reason alone, I couldn't do it. Even if it was only two days, I never wanted her to forget me. Because I sure as shit could never forget her.

Stepping back, I pushed her hair over her shoulder, my fingers fumbling with the two small hooks that fastened her bra. I worked it one way and then the other, but it wouldn't budge. Giving up, I raked a hand through my hair.

"I can't figure this fucking thing out. I'm about to rip it off."

Lily's shoulders quaked, her throaty laugh filling the room.

"It's not funny." Crushing her back to my chest, I growled in her ear, "I was making a grand gesture."

Turning, she held my gaze while she reached behind her and unfastened the hooks with ease. She slid the lavender straps off her shoulders, holding the strip of fabric at her side. I had her on her back on the bed before it hit the ground.

"So beautiful." As I swirled my tongue over one nipple, it hardened to a stiff peak, while I rolled the other between my fingers. She arched off the bed, groaning loudly when I grazed the tender tip with my teeth.

I moved down her stomach, planting kisses as I went. Dropping to my knees on the floor, I pulled her to the end of the bed. Propped on her elbows, she widened her eyes in near panic.

"Cameron," she said breathlessly, her chest heaving, "you can't...I've never..." She slammed her knees shut like a vice.

I swallowed hard, while my heart skipped a beat. No way.

"Baby, you're not..." The word clogged in my throat.

Her eyes grew wider. "No!" She sat bolt upright. "I'm twenty-three years old; I'm not a virgin. I've just never...nobody's ever done that." Turning her face away, her cheeks flushed crimson.

She was serious.

"What?" The shock rocked me back on my heels. "I mean... how?"

Crossing her arms over her chest, she lifted her chin. "My ex-boyfriend...he just didn't, ok?"

Too many years of discussing sex openly—what I wanted, what a girl wanted to give me— had destroyed any filter that might have existed.

"So none of your boyfriends..." I furrowed my brow. "*Ever?*"

What kind of idiots had she been dating?

"There's only been one. We met in high school." She hugged herself tighter at the admission. "He left...I mean, we broke up when I left the business program and switched to art."

My hand moved to her leg, rubbing the back of her calf absently.

"You were a business major?"

"Yes," she sighed, clasping her hands in her lap. "I was in the business program. But I hated it."

Defeat was written all over her. Chase had studied business at Stanford. He was the smartest guy I knew, but he had crawled into a hole and studied his ass off to get the degree.

"Was it hard?" Grabbing her hands, I pulled her to the floor, settling her on my lap. "My brother went to business school. He said it was a bitch."

"It wasn't hard." She sighed again. "Telling my parents? That was hard. I've always been a disappointment. But dropping out was more than they could deal with. We've only spoken a few times in the last two years."

She looked lost. And the urge to comfort her was strong. Too strong to resist. Pulling her to my chest, I let my hand run down the length of her hair.

"How could you ever be a disappointment?" As I sifted through the golden strands, I felt her shudder.

"M-my stutter, for one. My dad kinda felt bad about that. But my mom—she thought it was my fault," she said while peering up at me, "that I didn't try hard enough to be n-normal."

Normal.

"You're not normal. Why would you want to be?" Gripping her tighter when she stiffened, I kissed the top of her head. "You're special."

"Special, huh?" She chuckled. "I hate that word. My m-mom used to tell everyone about my 's-special' classes. Getting accepted to SMU and maintaining a stellar GPA still wasn't enough to convince her I'm not stupid."

I barked out a laugh.

"You're far from stupid. Just because you do that cute little thing when you get nervous?" Looking up at me in disbelief, she studied my face, stripping away layer after layer of my defenses. I shifted uncomfortably before continuing. "I barely graduated. My dad hauled me around to every bar in Austin until he left my junior year. Even got me my own fake ID."

"Why would he do that?" The disbelief in her eyes softened

to concern, prompting me to continue. Tucking a strand of hair behind her ear, I blew out a breath.

"Because my old man didn't give a shit if we grunted like animals as long as we did it with a guitar in our hands."

I shrugged, trying for casual to avoid the next emotion that crept over her face. Pity. I didn't do pity. But then I didn't do sharing, and here I was naked on the floor telling this woman the Cliff Notes version of my life story. But somehow, I couldn't help myself, so I continued.

"He shit a brick when Chase got accepted to Stanford. Thought it was a waste of time. He left after that. Just didn't come home one day. I didn't see him again until my first single hit the charts."

Burying her head under my chin, she pressed her cheek to my chest. Truthfully, I expected more questions. But I was jaded. People were always pumping me for information. Looking for a story.

"Do you miss him?" she whispered.

"My dad?"

She nodded against my chest.

"Fuck, NO." I snorted. "He was an asshole. My brother did more to raise me than that man ever did."

"I miss my parents. Not all the time, but Christmas…and my birthday." Pulling away, she looked down, her hair falling over her face, so all I could see was the tip of her nose. "Last Christmas I ordered a turkey from the grocery store. I had to eat turkey sandwiches for two weeks. I blew my budget on that damn bird."

Sliding my hand to the nape of her neck, I titled her face up to me.

"When's the last time you saw them?"

"A couple months ago. The Tennison Foundation dedicated the new library at SMU. I didn't talk to them."

The Tennison Foundation?

"You're a Tennison?" My hand froze, my fingers still twisted in her hair.

Lily slapped my chest. "I know you have a lot of women, but you could at least act like you remember my last name."

64

"I know your last name." My back went stiff in defense. "I just didn't know you were—"

"Marcus Tennison's daughter?" she finished, looking up to gauge my reaction. "Why? Because I drive a beat up Honda and work at The Mansion?" She arched a brow. "Yeah, I could see how that would throw you."

The Tennisons were Texas elite. Hell, they were elite, period. To think Marcus Tennison, land baron and philanthropist, had anything in common with Tyler Noble, a washed-up drunk who abandoned his family. Marcus may not have left, but he abandoned Lily just the same. At least I had Chase.

Her hand went to my face, startling me out of my thoughts.

"What's the matter?" Her eyes were full of concern.

"Nothing. I was just thinking." I smoothed away the crease on her forehead. "You don't have any brothers or sisters?"

The smile on her face was wistful.

"No, just me. Although, my mom told me plenty of times she wished *that* was different. I thought if I could be successful, do something with my art, maybe," she shrugged, her voice dropping to a whisper, "she'd like me more."

I knew that feeling. Knew it all too well. Drowning myself in music and the adoration that went with it—I pushed it aside most of the time.

Lowering her to the floor, I placed her arms over her head, holding both her wrists easily with one hand. She arched her back to meet my touch as I skimmed her breasts, her stomach, and her creamy thighs. My stomach coiled with want. For all of her. The vulnerable girl that was just curled on my lap ,and the one below me now. Her knees fell open when I reached between her legs.

I swallowed her gasp, caressing her tongue gently as I pushed a finger into her slick core. Her wrists strained against my restraint as I bent to take her nipple into my mouth. Coaxing her legs wider, I slid a second finger inside, teasing her clit with my thumb as I pumped them in and out gently. My name tumbled out of her mouth, her hips moving to meet my thrusts.

I could lose it right here, climb on top of her, and fling us both over the edge.

"Let me taste you, Lily." The hoarse whisper was almost a plea.

She nodded, her eyes screwed shut as she ground against my fingers. I released her wrists, and she whimpered softly when I withdrew and reached behind me for a pillow from the bed.

Moving between her legs, I bit back a groan at the sight of her completely spread out in front of me.

"Lift your hips, baby."

Shoving the pillow under her, I dropped to my stomach, just inches from her. The carpet was rough against my throbbing cock, but I couldn't think past her silky skin. All for me. My hand splayed over her stomach, holding her in place when my tongue swept her clit. I circled her slowly, and she cried out when I pushed one finger and then another deep inside. Threading her fingers in my hair, she slammed against me with every thrust. I moved my hand from her stomach, letting her move freely. Finding her other hand grasping the pillow, I pried it free, lacing our fingers. She looked down with wide eyes, panting and moaning through parted lips.

"Cam—I'm going to—fuck." Squeezing her eyes shut, she threw her head back, her groans incoherent and guttural.

I stroked her deep inside, sucking her clit until every muscle clenched. Her fingers tightened in my hair, pulling me farther into her as she broke apart, calling my name. My name. As she relaxed against the pillow, I drew out a final wave, making a long sweep over her center as I withdrew my fingers. I rose to my knees, taking her other hand to pull her into a sitting position.

"Come to bed, pretty girl."

She was stunned into silence, and I almost laughed at the innocent look on her face.

"Okay."

She pushed to her feet, and I steadied her when her knees wobbled, scattering the pillows when I threw the covers back and nudged her between the sheets. I crawled in after her, turning to flip off the light.

All night. She was going to be here all night. Excitement

coursed through me with a hint of something else. Fear. Trepidation.

Reaching for me, she wrapped herself around me in the dark, seeking out my mouth with hers. I pulled her on top of me, deepening the kiss until my cock throbbed, begging for release.

Her hair brushed my face as she sat up and fumbled around on the nightstand. I could just make out the foil package when she brought it to her mouth, ripping it open with her teeth. Jerking my hips in surprise when she took me in her hand, I felt the condom slide down my length. My arms fell around her when she lowered herself on top of me.

"How do you want me?" Her warm breath danced across my lips.

In one movement, I reversed our positions so I was above her. Pressing my forehead against hers, I tasted the honey of her lips.

"Any way I can get you."

CHAPTER 10

"You can't cancel!" Lily whirled around the room, long strands of her wet hair sticking to her face. "Where's my bra? I can't find my—"

Pulling it from beneath the bed, I held it up, arching a brow at her. "Calm down, darlin'."

Stalking toward me with her arms crossed over her chest, she stopped when her knees hit mine. "Give it to me."

Wrapping my arms around her, I fell back against the mattress.

"I'll give it to you all right." I nipped her neck, holding her tightly as she squirmed.

When I found the spot right below her ear, she giggled, kicking her legs out.

"Stop…Cameron…stop!" Her giggles gave way to shrieks of laughter.

Loosening my grip, I sucked her moist skin, the rumble in her throat vibrating against my lips.

"I'd rather just stay here."

Sliding my hand to her ass, I felt myself stir. Any pursuits outside this hotel room had suddenly lost their appeal.

"There's no way." She looked down to where our hips were

joined. "Not after last night and this morning."

Grinding against her, I proved just how wrong she was, but I released her anyway.

I was surprised myself. Twice last night and once in the shower this morning was a record, even for me.

"Believe me, I could." I dipped my fingers in the waistband of the boxers she was wearing. My boxers. "But I won't."

I stroked her back when she sat up and was disappointed when she slipped the bra over her shoulders.

"You know," I said as I twisted a strand of her wet hair around my finger absently, "I only bought that package to impress you."

"You did what?" She turned to me in shock.

"Sue me." I fell back on my elbows, giving her a sly smile. "I wanted to spend some time alone with you. Totally worth it."

Standing, she snatched her jeans off the floor. "You could have asked," she said, teetering as she pulled them on. "You didn't have to spend ten thousand dollars to get me to go out with you."

"That's good to know." Sitting up, I snaked an arm around her waist, pulling her between my legs. "I'd have to cancel all our dates in Dallas if I had to drop that kind of cash every time I'm passing through."

I bit my tongue as soon as the words left my mouth.

She blinked, her expression going blank, except for the tell-tale crease on her brow.

"Lily..."

Turning, she grabbed her purse and headed for the bathroom. "Get dressed, mister," she called over her shoulder in an overly cheery tone. "I've never had someone spend that kind of cash for the pleasure of my company. I'm not going to miss a single minute of it."

Dropping my head in my hands, I groaned. *Stupid, stupid.* I glanced at the clock for the hundredth time. It started last night when I woke up with Lily pressed against me. I looked at the damn clock and unease settled over me. When I rolled her over and buried myself inside her, I chased it away.

My phone lit up, Nirvana's "All Apologies" filling the room. Sighing, I swiped my finger over the screen.

"What's up, Logan?"

"You still in your room?"

"Yeah. We're…I'm heading out soon."

"Who's we?" He snorted a laugh. "Never mind…ditch the bitch, we got to head out to Arlington."

"I told you, I'm out today," I muttered. "I did the interview with Wendy, and—"

Laughter erupted on the other end. "That's fucking perfect, man. Is Wendy still there? I had to cancel a shit load of interviews today to get this sound check done. If Wendy can come and do an on the spot promo, that would be great. Plus, you could probably nail her in the limo on the way back."

I winced, my stomach roiling at the thought of Wendy. "Dude, it's not Wendy." I lowered my voice when Lily walked in. She got down on her knees and lifted the dust ruffle on the bed. "I told you I have plans today."

I reached down and cupped her ass. She swatted my hand away.

"You're going to have to cancel," he said. "That fucking stadium is a beast. There are lighting issues, acoustic issues. The Jumbotron alone is the biggest one in the country."

Raking a hand through my hair, I looked down at Lily, seated on the floor putting on the pink Converse she must have been searching for.

"All right," I muttered, "but this isn't an all-day thing. I'm not doing interviews. Don't even ask, Logan."

She looked up at me, her concern growing deeper by the second.

"Do you want to share a limo? Chloe said—"

"No," I snapped, "I told you I'd be there, and I will."

Hitting the end button, I threw the phone on the bed and paced with my fingers laced behind my head.

"What's wrong?" Lily was on her feet, standing in front of me.

Blowing out a breath, I shook my head. "Lily, I'm so sorry," I began.

Stepping back, she crossed her arms.

"I've got to go to Arlington. There's a sound check. Something isn't right with the acoustics. I really wanted—"

Placing a hand on my arm, she cut off my rambling apology. "It's cool. I'll cancel it." She winced. "There's going to be a penalty. I'll try to talk them out of it, but I don't know."

My shoulders relaxed, all the tension leaving me.

"Don't cancel the whole thing. I still want to take you to the museum tomorrow." Lacing our fingers, I kissed the back of her hand. "And the ballet tomorrow night. I promise."

"You don't have to make any promises. We'll just see how it goes." Lifting up on her tiptoes, she pecked my lips. "Let me get my stuff so you can get out of here."

"You're going with me." I maneuvered around her to root around for a clean t-shirt and jeans in my open suitcase.

"No, I'm not." She grabbed her panties off the floor and threw them in her purse.

"Why not?" I stepped into a pair of jeans and pulled a black t-shirt over my head. "We can get something to eat afterward."

It had never crossed my mind that she wouldn't be staying with me tonight. And tomorrow. I glanced at the clock again, my stomach tumbling. Crossing the room, I sat on the edge of the bed and pulled on my socks.

"I don't have any clothes here," she said, pulling down the waistband of her jeans. "I'm wearing your boxers, for Christ's sake."

She was fucking adorable when she got flustered. Between the pink in her cheeks and her expressive brow, she'd never last one minute at the poker tables in Vegas.

Grabbing her hips, I pulled her forward until I was eye level with her chest. I moved my hands down the outside of her thighs and back up, taking my t-shirt that she was wearing along for the ride. Planting a kiss on her breast, I caught her nipple between my teeth when it hardened, holding her tighter when she squirmed.

"Just knowing you're wearing my boxers. That they're right

72

here," running a hand over the front of her jeans, I slid it between her thighs and rubbed, "is about the sexiest fucking thing I can imagine. I'm getting hard just thinking about it." Kissing the other breast, I grabbed her hand and pulled it to my crotch. "Don't make me go all the way to Arlington with a hard-on, baby."

She tugged my hair, pulling my face up to look at her. "How's it going to be any better if I go to Arlington with you?"

Rubbing my chin across the top of her breast, I reached around and cupped her ass. "Arlington is almost an hour away. Have you ever had sex in a limo, Lily?"

Lily insisted on sneaking out the side door and waiting in her car. Searching the parking lot, I pushed open the door of the limo, and Lily jumped out of her car, nearly bowling me over as she climbed in. Pulling the door closed, I moved toward her on the seat. She fell backward, locking her legs around my waist. Leaning over her, I hit the intercom button.

"Yes, Mr. Knight."

"I'm on a conference call." Swallowing hard, I looked down at Lily. My pants were open, and her hand was inside. "Ah…no interruptions. No exceptions."

"Very good, Mr. Knight."

With one tug of my belt loops, she had my jeans and boxers around my knees and my cock in her mouth. Groaning, I grabbed the seat, digging my free hand in her hair. She gripped my base, stroking and sucking until my stomach coiled.

"Lily."

She lifted her hooded eyes, sucking harder.

"Baby, please," I clenched my teeth, fighting the urge to give in and let go.

Releasing me, she pursed her lips. "What's the matter? Am I not doing it right?"

Falling back on the seat, I pulled her forward until she was straddling me. "Of course, you're doing it right." I pushed the hair off her face. "Too fucking right. I'm going to come in less than a minute if you keep that up."

"Isn't that the point?" Her hand wandered between us, and she grabbed me again.

"That's one point." Reaching down, I pulled off her shoes, giving her a sly smile. "I've got something better in mind."

Sliding to the floorboard, she shrugged off her jeans while I grabbed the condom I had stowed in my front pocket and shoved my pants around my ankles. She watched me roll the condom on, yipping when I pulled her up to sit astride me.

I grabbed the hem of her shirt, pulling it over her head without taking it off. Fisting the fabric behind her back, I locked her arms in place, my eyes never leaving hers. Yanking one of her breasts free, I gripped the t-shirt tighter, holding her in place as I clamped onto her erect nipple. Stilling her arms, she pushed her chest forward, whimpering softly when I pulled back to barely skim my tongue over the hardened peak. Fisting my shaft, I scooted forward a fraction until I was at her entrance, sliding the head back and forth over her slick center. I groaned loudly when she sank down on top of me, taking me to the hilt.

Releasing her arms when her eyes went wide, I grabbed her hips. She slid her eyes shut, biting her lip until it lost color.

"Baby, open your eyes."

They fluttered open, locking on mine as she rolled her hips. Wrapping my arms completely around her, I laced our fingers behind her back. She lowered her forehead to mine, increasing the pace until she was slamming into me with every thrust.

Her pants heated my face, her brow going slick with sweat.

"I-I…Cameron…"

"Kiss me, baby."

Her mouth was on mine, our tongues twisting and tangling as the first wave hit her. Her lips slid off mine as she groaned, slowing her rhythm to a grind when she broke apart, clenching my cock relentlessly.

"Yes…yes…" she mumbled, riding me into the ground.

"Lily…" I growled when the first spasm of my release hit

me. "You feel it…Fuck, baby."

She was all around me. She was everywhere and everything. My mouth was on her neck, breathing her in and tasting her as I pushed so far inside I didn't ever want to leave. Loosening my grip, I rested my forehead against her shoulder, the sights and sounds and movement of our surroundings dragging me back to the now.

Pulling her back when she went to move, I held her tight. "Stay," I breathed.

Stay with me. Today. Tomorrow.

I tried to see beyond that. But I couldn't.

CHAPTER 11

When I clamped my hand down on Lily's bobbing leg, she looked up at me and smiled nervously.

"This won't take long," I said, hoping like hell I was right.

The limo pulled to a stop in the shadow of the largest stadium I'd ever seen. Squinting, Lily looked out the tinted window, craning her neck.

"You're playing here?"

"Not just us, darlin'." Sliding on my sunglasses, I shifted in my seat at the sight of the news vans parked a few yards away. "There are six bands. We're mid lineup."

Nodding, she looked out again.

"Just a few more minutes, Mr. Knight," the driver cut in over the intercom. "We're waiting on security. There's a lot of press around."

Groaning, I pressed the intercom button. "Thanks."

"Cameron, I'm not comfortable with this." Lily scooted back against the seat. "I'm just going to stay here."

"You can't stay here." I chuckled, grabbing her hand. "It'll be fine. You're with me."

My smile fell away when Lily looked over at me, brutal honesty shading her blue eyes.

"I'm glad I'm the girl that's getting the Cameron Knight treatment this week, but I could have done without this excursion. It only reminds me that this is a game to you," she said quietly. "It makes it harder for me to pretend."

Swallowing hard over the bitter taste in my mouth, I squeezed her hand. "Pretend what, Lily?"

She gave me a watery smile. "Pretend that I'm not just a girl you're killing time with between shows."

I could tell her that's how it started. Make it clear that it was different now. But in the real world, it wasn't worth the risk. The risk of broken promises and messy complications.

Pushing a hand through my hair, I rested my arm on the back of the seat, sliding on a mask of indifference.

"There's nobody I'd rather be killing time with than you, Lily."

She nodded her head, the smile never fading. It was frozen on her face, masking the sting of the callous words that rolled off my tongue effortlessly.

An awkward silence stretched between us, so unpalatable it twisted my stomach. It felt like we were waiting for ten hours instead of ten minutes.

Entwining our fingers when the limo door swung open, I anchored her to me, making a promise that I couldn't speak out loud. For the rest of our time together, Lily would never see Cameron Knight again.

Pushing through the first wave of photographers, I slipped my arm over Lily's shoulder. She burrowed closer to my side, her eyes on the ground, and her face turned into my chest. The paparazzi began their taunting and prodding when it was apparent I wasn't in the mood for a chat.

"Cameron! Who's the flavor of the week?"

"Look over here, sweetheart! Say cheese."

"Who's the hot piece, Cam?"

Lily shuddered, her steps faltering as she tried to keep up.

"I'm sorry, baby." My voice rose over the taunts. "Just a few more steps."

What the fuck was with all the media? Ninety percent of the time there was nobody at the venue. In the distance, I saw Lindsey with her arms folded over her chest, a smirk tilting up one corner of her mouth. In my haste to get to the field, I nearly plowed down a photographer that stepped in front of me. I'd seen the guy before. He was notorious for getting the best pictures. Candid shots of celebrities spewing obscenities or lunging at him.

Pointing the camera at Lily, he whistled. "Show me your tits, sweetheart. I'll make you famous," he jeered, his camera clicking frame after frame.

Lily's head snapped up, her eyes going wide as the color drained from her face.

"You motherfucker!" I roared.

Lily's hand clamped down on my arm when I lurched forward. The photographer snickered, hiding behind the camera as he swung it in my direction.

"Cameron—don't." She stepped in front of me. "This piece of shit is just trying to get under your skin."

Squaring her shoulders, she pulled me forward, sliding her hand down my arm until our fingers were linked. I kept my eyes on the back of her head, a smile blooming on my face. She was amazing, this girl.

Grinding to a stop, I pulled her backward, her mouth dropping open in shock when I spun her around.

"Come here, you." Ignoring the shutters clicking, I crushed my mouth to hers.

It took her a second to yield, to allow me this one gesture. I wasn't hiding her in the dark. I wanted her with me in the light.

Breaking away from Lily's mouth at the tug on my sleeve, I looked down at the perfectly manicured hand. Lindsey's face was a mask of barely contained fury.

"Come on," she hissed, pushing past the photographers,

who scattered as we walked.

They got what they wanted. The money shot. Pulling Lily to my side, I dropped my hand to her waist, stroking the skin at her side as we walked.

"Good job, baby." I planted a kiss on her temple.

"Wh—what the fuck was that?" Lily mumbled, startling a laugh out of me. "Are they always so…obnoxious?"

"Nah. They just wanted a couple pictures of the prettiest girl out here."

She snorted, her shoulders relaxing as we made our way across the field.

"Who's that?" she whispered, lifting her chin to indicate Lindsey's back.

"The wicked witch of the west, or as she's more commonly known in the business, Lindsey Barger." I looked down at Lily, arching a brow. "Our manager."

Logan brushed past Lindsey like she wasn't there and strode toward us.

"Hey man, it's fucking crazy out there, right?" He ground to a halt, his gaze flickering from me to Lily. "Hey, Lily. It's good to see you again." Leaning over, he brushed a kiss on her cheek.

"Hi, Logan." She gave him a brilliant smile. "How's it going?"

"Can't complain." He moved to her side as we walked toward the group of chairs in front of the stage.

Pulling her toward me instinctively, I leveled Logan with a scowl when I met his gaze.

Smirking, he lifted a brow. I was more than willing to pummel him to the ground and give him a taste of the AstroTurf if he didn't behave.

The smirk turned into a smile as he ambled along, whistling to himself. Sean and Christian were seated in the front row with their heads together when we walked up.

"Hey, asshole, about time you showed up," Sean said, doing a double take when he noticed Lily at my side. He jumped up. "Fuck, Lily, I didn't see you." Mimicking Logan's earlier gesture, he leaned in and pecked her on the cheek.

What the fuck was with these guys? They didn't have manners, let alone chivalry.

"Hi, Sean," Lily said, an adorable flush creeping into her cheeks. "Good to see you."

She turned to Christian, reaching out a hand. "I'm Lily," she said cheerily.

Taking her hand, Christian's gaze shifted to mine. "Nice to meet you, Lily," his lip twitching as he held back a grin.

Pulling her back to my side and out of their clutches, I reached under her shirt, splaying my hand on her stomach possessively. My heart was thumping, beating wildly against my ribs, despite my casual demeanor.

Logan looked down at my hand. He saw right through me. Saw what I was hiding. They all did.

"Caged—you've got thirty minutes." The guy with the headset at the center of the stage motioned for us to come up.

All of our gear was set. The guys headed for the stage while I lingered for a second with Lily. I caught Logan peeking at me over his shoulder.

"This won't take long." Turning to follow the guys, I spun around and impulsively pulled her to me for a kiss, lifting her until her feet dangled off the ground.

Her tongue wrapped around mine gently, in that way of hers. Calming me. If I could bottle it, have it with me always, I swear I would.

"God, you're sweet," I said, easing her to her feet.

"Right back at you." She gave me a playful shove. "Now go to work, Mr. Knight."

My stomach tightened. Lily wouldn't be able to pick out Cameron Knight on the street. In the time I'd known her, he'd barely made an appearance.

CHAPTER 12

A gain!" Logan shouted, glaring at me over his shoulder. I
was looking across the field to where Lindsey and Lily were
having a heated discussion. They stood toe-to-toe, with Lindsey
towering over Lily in her five inch heels. Lily's arms were folded
over her chest, her mouth set in a thin line.

Since I missed the opening cue, Logan stalked over to me.
"What the fuck is going on, Cam?" He followed my gaze to the
two women, his tone softening. "What's the dragon lady talking
to Lily about?"

"Who knows?" I shrugged. "Let's get this done."

Logan hesitated for a second, studying me before he walked
back to center stage. Letting my mind go blank, I turned my back
and felt the music, blending the opening chords with Christian's
drum beat to perfection. Logan's vocals rose up and filled the
stadium, accompanied by Sean's pounding bass. It was my song
we were playing. My words and my arrangement.

Even in the light of day, the changing lights that kept time
with the music spurred me on. Turning to Logan, I caught the
glint in his eye. The same infectious spark that had brought us
together years ago. Ambling over to him, I wailed into the mic,
harmonizing easily. A group of girls stood off to the side of the

stage. Groupies that showed up on the tour buses of the smaller bands who weren't lucky enough to get hotel rooms. Strutting toward them, I smiled seductively, grinding my hips as the music poured out.

Logan joined me, vying for their attention. I playfully shoved him away, locking eyes with a girl that shoved her way to the front, shaking her hair and bouncing on the balls of her feet. Turning to her friend, they fused their hips and swayed to the music while they stole glances at Logan and me.

Closing my eyes, I played the final refrain, drawing out the last chord until it died on my strings.

"Fuck yeah!" Logan slapped me on the back. "That was it! It sounds awesome in here. Let's wrap it. Whoa—check out the Jumbotron."

My mouth fell open when I looked to midfield. On the biggest screen I'd ever seen, my image was frozen, staring down at the girls with a "fuck me now" look, hot enough to melt butter.

My gaze fell to Lily, seated at the front of the stage. Lindsey was beside her, the smile on her face so malicious I wanted to strangle her.

Pulling the strap off my shoulder, I handed it to the roadie and walked toward the ramp. Lily's eyes followed me, her face impassive and unreadable. Chewing up the space that separated us, I walked straight to her, avoiding Lindsey when I stopped.

"You ready?" I said, shoving my hand out for her to take.

Lily blinked, her gaze dropping from my face to my outstretched hand.

Take my hand, baby.

She reached out hesitantly, and I pulled her up, breathing a sigh of relief.

"Cameron," Lindsey said, teetering to her feet when I didn't acknowledge her. "If you don't return my calls, I can't schedule any interviews or rehearsals," she scolded. "Haven't you gotten any of my messages?"

Lily's hand went limp as I stalked across the field with her behind me.

"Cameron!"

Stopping at Lindsey's bellow, I turned and walked toward her.

"We just rehearsed; we're tight," I snapped. "We're done until the show. Christian needs his rest."

Lindsey chuckled. "Christian looks fine to me."

"I'll see you Saturday. Contact Logan if you need anything."

Lindsey grabbed my arm, her nails digging in just enough to let me know she was serious.

"You have responsibilities, Cameron. We have a meet and greet tonight." Her heated gaze shifted to Lily. "Time to stop *dicking around* and get back to work."

Shaking loose of her grasp, I turned on my heel, nearly bowling over the two girls that had been watching the rehearsal from the side of the stage. The dark-haired girl, obviously the bolder of the two, looked up at me, putting a hand on my chest.

"Hey, Cameron." She ran her tongue along her bottom lip seductively. "That was fucking brilliant. You guys are phenomenal."

"Thanks. That's good to hear." Smiling tightly, I stepped around them. "You girls have a good day."

Her hand fell to my arm. "We could make sure you have a really good day." She slipped her other arm around her friend's waist, pulling her flush to her side. "Let's go find someplace to party."

"I don't think so. I have plans."

She licked her lips again. "No problem. We don't mind sharing."

"No thanks." Tightening my grip on Lily's hand, I brushed past them, power-walking the length of the field. She struggled behind me, trying to keep my pace.

"Cameron."

I kept moving, trying to put some distance between us and the fucked up mess at our back.

"Cameron!" She ground to a halt midfield, grabbing the back of my shirt.

I turned a heated gaze on her, full of irritation mixed with something else. Embarrassment. For her. For me.

Lily's gaze was just as heated, her normally pink cheeks stained deep crimson.

"What?" I bit out.

"What?" she barked. "Look, if you want to go with those girls, feel free. *You* asked me to come. Don't drag me out of here like I'm a dog that pissed on your carpet."

"I—I don't want to go anywhere with them. I…It's just…" Shaking my head, I looked down. "I don't know what to say. I didn't mean to embarrass you."

My head snapped up when she laughed.

"You didn't." She snickered. "Until you dragged me away like you couldn't wait to find the nearest bus stop."

I blinked at her, certain I didn't hear her right. How could she think I was mad at anyone but myself? Rubbing the back of my neck, I looked up, hoping the right words would fall from the sky.

Lily stepped forward, the tips of her Converse meeting my boots.

"You can tell me, Cameron. Whatever it is."

Tell her what? Tell her I want to take her to Austin and introduce her to my brother. Tell her I want to go rafting with her down the Guadeloupe and sleep with her under the stars. Tell her I want to see if this can last longer than two days, but I can't promise that it will.

"Those girls—they didn't mean anything. The song. When I play, the audience, they're like props. I didn't even realize…"

Reaching down, she took my hands. They relaxed immediately, sliding between her fingers and locking in place.

"You didn't realize what?" She arched a brow, a smile playing across her lips. "That you're sexy as hell, and every chick out here wants you to play them like you play that guitar? Hell, even I was ready to jump you."

I laughed. "You wanted to jump me, huh?"

"Don't judge."

Pulling her to me with our joined hands behind her back, I placed a soft kiss on her mouth. Her fingers wiggled.

"I'm beginning to think this is a thing with you, Cameron."

"What's a thing?"

"This." She wiggled her fingers again. "First you tangle me up in my t-shirt while you're having your way with me, and now you've got my hands twisted behind my back. If you want to tie me up, just ask."

Dropping her hands, I cupped the back of her neck, pulling her forward until she was on her tip toes, her mouth so close to mine, her breath heated my lips.

"You better be careful, baby. I might take you up on that."

She wrapped her arms around my neck, sliding a hand in my hair. A twinge of pain shot through me when she coiled her fingers in the strands, pulling me to her neck.

"Promise," she breathed.

CHAPTER 13

Lily's back was against my chest, her legs spread out on the seat as she devoured the last of her What-a-Burger. Half of my burger sat untouched on the seat next to me. My appetite was basically non-existent. On the other hand, Lily was poking around inside the bag, foraging for leftover fries and onion rings.

I chuckled.

My mama always told me never to trust any woman that didn't appreciate good barbecue or a greasy cheeseburger. I didn't rely much on her dating advice since she was leery of anyone that resided west of El Paso. She was thoroughly convinced that Texas was a country unto itself, with everything you could ever want available inside its borders.

"It's the largest state for a reason, sugar plum," she always said.

When I found out in the third grade that Alaska was actually larger, I couldn't wait to share the information.

"That's rubbish," she'd scolded, the normally serene pools of her eyes turning fierce. "I don't know what they're teaching you, but if I ever hear you say that again, I've got a bar of soap with your name on it."

Of course, Callie, my sainted mother, was the same woman

who believed the sun rose and set on Tyler Noble's ass. Her judgment was questionable at best.

"Did you get enough to eat, darlin'?" I gave Lily a wary look.

She had the bag upturned, gathering the crumbs from the onion rings in her palm.

Looking over her shoulder at me sheepishly, she brushed the crumbs off her hands.

"I'm fine. I just love burgers and fries." She sighed. "I wasn't allowed to eat them when I was a kid. I guess they're like forbidden fruit."

Brushing the crumbs off her lap, she downed the last of her water and threw the bottle in the bag. She scooted off the seat, crawling toward the mini fridge. Damned if I wasn't right on the money when I told her that having her wear my boxers was about the sexiest thing I'd ever seen. The black elastic waistband peeking out of her jeans brought my cock to life faster than the porn that Logan played on a loop on the tour bus.

"Want something?"

You...now.

"Nope. I'm good." I smiled, trying to figure out how to keep her in that position long enough to get her pants off.

"Are you sure?" Her brow creased in the most adorable way.

"Positive."

My phone lit up on the seat. I'd set it to vibrate after Logan's third call. Lily crawled toward me, settling on the floorboard between my knees. Twisting a hand in her hair, I tugged it gently until she stared up at me, a wide smile on her face.

"There's enough seats in this thing for twelve people," I joked. "You don't have to sit on the floor."

She turned sideways, resting her head on my knee.

"My dad...he had a limo just like this." Her smile lost a little shine at the memory. "We never had a car when I was growing up. My mother used to get so mad at me because I loved to crawl around on the floor." Shrugging, she looked down. "I don't get to ride around in limos anymore. I guess it just reminds me of my childhood."

"I never rode in a limo until we signed with a record label." Stroking her hair, I fanned it out over my jeans. "I didn't even ride in a limo to the prom."

She propped her elbow on my knee, her eyes going wide. "Tell me about your prom."

"Not much to tell." Tracing my index finger down her cheek, I brushed it along her bottom lip. "I'm sure it was just like yours. Except, maybe you didn't have to ride there in your best friend's twenty year old pickup truck."

Actually, I couldn't really complain about that. Logan's tiny Ford had a single bench seat, assuring that my date for the evening was on my lap for the entire ride. Who knows if I would have had the nerve to go all the way if Crystal hadn't taken the initiative after having my cock pressed against her all the way home?

"I didn't have a prom. I came out when I was sixteen," Lily said, resting her cheek on her hand. "I went to Hockaday."

"I have no idea what you're talking about, darlin', but if you're telling me you were a lesbian until you were sixteen, I'd be happy to explore that with you." I waggled my brows.

"You perv." Lily bit the inside of my jean-clad thigh.

"Ouch!" Grabbing her under the arms, I pulled her onto my lap. "No biting—unless we're naked." I kissed the tip of her nose. "What's Hockaday? And tell me all about coming out. Don't spare any details."

"It's not that sexy. Hockaday's an all-girls school. I had my 'coming out' party when I was sixteen." Puzzled at my confused expression, she stared at me. "You know, a debutante ball? Big-ass hoop skirts? Boring guys with crew cuts?"

I'd heard about debutante balls. But I didn't know they actually still had them. And again, my only experience with all-girls schools was courtesy of Logan's vast porn stash.

"Sounds fancy." Pulling her legs up so she was completely on my lap, I settled back in the seat. "Who took you to this big 'coming out' party?"

She shifted uncomfortably, staring down at her fingernails. I closed my hands over hers. "You can tell me," I cajoled. "Did he have a hump? Three nipples? Or a—"

"No," she snapped, cutting me off. "He was just a regular asshole. No deformities. Unless you count arrogance and an underdeveloped personality."

"I was just kidding, darlin'." Resting my chin on her shoulder, I gave her a squeeze. "Just make me a list of any of your old boyfriends. I'll take care of them for you."

"I told you before, Cameron, there was only one guy. Ever. One fucking asshole."

She finally looked up, noting my shocked expression.

"What? Big surprise!" Scooting off my lap to the far end of the seat, she folded her arms across her chest. "I'm nothing like you. My parents didn't let me go to parties or dances. And my only boyfriend—no, my fiancé—broke up with me because he didn't want to be married to an 'artist.'" Dropping her head to the back of the seat, she stared out the sunroof.

Chuckling to myself, I shook my head. Lily turned to me, fury igniting in her eyes.

"It's not funny, Cameron."

The band tightened in my chest at the sight of her trembling chin.

"Lily…" I scooted to her side, but she refused to look at me.

Dropping to my knees on the floorboard, I pried open her legs and positioned myself between her knees. I grabbed her calves when she tried to pull her legs away.

"Let me go."

Wrapping her legs around my waist, I held them there until she looked at me.

"Darlin', I wasn't laughing at you." Kneading the outside of her legs, I took a calming breath before I continued. "I was laughing because when I was growing up, I thought people like you, like your family, didn't have any problems. My old man would go on a bender and leave for days at a time. Sometimes my mom had to go to the neighbors to 'borrow' a loaf of bread to make us toast with sugar. For *dinner*."

Her legs fell away when I let them go, turning until my back was against the seat. It felt good to share a bit of my past with someone without fear it would make its way into some D-list gossip column. Too good.

Reaching for a distraction, I grabbed my phone and listened to the voicemail from Logan. He ticked off the name of the club in Deep Ellum where the band was having the meet and greet. I opened the text and typed in a response.

I was complicating the situation. Muddying the water. And I couldn't help myself.

"Where do you live, darlin'?" I looked over my shoulder at Lily. "I thought we could swing by your place and pick up a few things. There's a thing tonight in Deep Ellum."

"I can't tonight." Her face fell, a forced smile appearing on her lips.

"Lily, I have two more days here." Taking her hand, I brushed my thumb against hers. "I'd like to spend them with you. Every minute."

"I'm sorry." She looked out the window, not meeting my gaze. "I have plans."

My stomach tumbled onto the floor at her feet, along with my pride.

"Can't you break them?"

For me.

"I can't."

"Suit yourself, darlin'."

Pulling my hand away, I checked the emails on my phone. Then I played Angry Birds. Then I just stared at the screen.

The limo finally, mercifully, pulled to a halt in front of The Mansion.

"Cameron?"

Her eyes were finally on me, but I was too pissed to look up. The driver swung the door open.

"I'm sorry. I have to—"

"No worries, Lily." Cutting her off, I looked up from my phone. "We were just killing time."

My smirk faded when her face went blank. She was out of the limo, running for her car before I could think.

Fuck.

Cursing, I hit the seat and jumped out.

"Lily!" I scanned the sea of cars.

My head swung in the direction of the engine that could only be hers. I moved toward it, but it was too late. She was out of the space, heading for the exit before I was halfway there.

CHAPTER 14

Sitting at the end of the couch in the VIP area, I nursed my second beer. This wasn't even my kind of club. My kind of crowd. The music was a loud and obnoxious blend of techno and pop. The only purpose it served, as far as I could tell, was to provide a beat so the girls that flocked around inside the velvet ropes could grind against each other.

Logan sipped his beer, his gaze trained on a couple of girls who had caught his attention. They weren't inside the VIP area, but just beyond the ropes. Logan motioned for Seth, the wall of muscle that doubled as security when he wasn't tearing down our equipment, to invite them inside.

Seth sauntered over to the pair, his hands drifting low on their hips when he drew them into a huddle. The willowy brunette looked over Seth's shoulder, licking her lips when she locked her gaze on Logan's. I didn't know exactly what kind of proposition was involved, but the slow smile that passed over Logan's lips was a pretty good indication.

"You want Betty or Veronica?"

Logan loved to throw in the reference to the blond and the brunette in the old Archie comics every chance he got. I think the dude must have used those comic books like porn when he was a kid. When I turned away, he swatted my leg.

"If you've got a thing for Lily, own it, son." He snorted. "You're the one that said she was a one and done."

"She is," I barked. "She just bailed a little earlier than I expected."

"Well then." Logan leaned back in his seat, watching the girls walk toward us, hand in hand. "Her replacement is coming off the line right now."

I looked up at the blond, who parked herself in front of me. She wasn't much of a replacement. It wasn't even a good dye job. Her dark roots gave her away.

"Take a seat, darlin'." Grabbing the brunette's hand, Logan pulled her down next to him. "I'm Logan. But you already know that, don't you?"

The brunette giggled, still holding on to her friend's hand.

"This broody fucker is Cameron." He locked his eyes on the blond, while the brunette wound her arm around his. "Why don't you see if you can lighten his mood?"

"I'm Candy," the blond said, wiggling between Logan and me on the couch.

Of course you are.

"Nice to meet you, Candy." Pushing to my feet, I drained my beer, looking anywhere but at her. "What's everybody drinking?"

Candy crossed her legs. "I'll take a shot." Licking her lips, she rubbed her foot up and down my calf. "I lose my mind when I do shots."

"Shots all around then!" Logan hooted.

I chewed the inside of my lip to keep from rolling my eyes. "Be right back." Putting my head down, I walked toward the bar.

"Four shots of Jack." Pressing my palms on the bar, I leaned forward, shouting loud enough to get the bartender's attention. He nodded.

"That didn't take long."

I turned to find Lindsey standing with her back against the bar, surveying the room.

"What are you talking about?" I reached into my pocket, throwing a twenty on the bar for a tip.

"I'll say this: she was pretty." Sipping her drink, she gave me a sidelong glance. "But she wasn't really your type, was she, Cam? I mean, she actually spoke in full sentences. Even had a few witty comebacks. It threw me a little."

My stomach flipped. Lindsey had spoken to Lily at the rehearsal. I never did find out what that was all about, but the burning in my gut told me it wasn't good.

"Oh yeah?" Grabbing one of the shots off the tray the bartender placed in front of me, I downed it. "What were the two of you chattering about?"

"Not much. I just told her to enjoy herself." Meeting my hard gaze, she took the red swizzle stick from her drink and swept her tongue over it. "While it lasts…"

While it lasts?

"Groupies…they all think they're 'the one.'" Lindsey snorted. "I told her to make sure she got cab fare tonight." Her gaze drifted to where Candy sat waiting across the room. "It's a good thing."

"She's not even here, Lindsey." I wished she were here. I wanted her to be here.

"Sure she is. I saw her ten minutes ago on the dance floor." Looking blandly at the partygoers outside the velvet rope, she dropped her swizzle stick back into the glass. "I figured you and your new friend chased her out of the VIP area."

The Jack splashed over the shot glasses when I dropped the tray on the bar. "It wasn't her. She doesn't even know where I am."

Lindsey's brow arched. "Of course she does."

"How would she—" As I whipped my head toward the dance floor, Lindsey's lilting laughter cut me off cold.

"I had to tell her." She waved her hand dismissively. "In case she was lucky enough to be photographed with you again, I wanted her dressed appropriately. That outfit she was wearing at the rehearsal was atrocious. And those pink sneakers? *Hideous.*" A smile curled her lips. "I'm sure they all look the same in the dark, but I can't have the public thinking you're banging a homeless girl."

Looking down at her hand when she patted my chest, I shrank at her touch.

"Don't give it a second thought." She sighed. "She's out of your hair. Let Chad worry about it."

"What's Chad have to do with it?"

"He's the one she was dancing with." She snorted derisively. "If you could call it dancing. It looked more like he was humping her leg. Chad has no—"

Before she could finish the thought, I was pushing my way through the small crowd, scanning every face. Ignoring Lindsey's booming voice at my back, I worked my way to the end of the VIP area. The blood pounding in my ears drowned out the music. Gripping the railing, I searched the dance floor, spotting Chad Dyer's tangled mess of black hair. He was the drummer for Crimson Five, a D-list boy band that somehow made its way on the ticket when one of the more seasoned groups dropped out of the tour.

I could barely make out the shape of the girl he was hunched over. My blood heated under my skin, scalding my insides, when I saw Lily's long, blond hair whipping from side to side as Chad shimmied down her body.

Seth grabbed my arm when I shoved past the velvet rope.

"What's up?" he said, alarm written all over his face. "Cam—"

Shrugging out of his grip, I waded into the crowd, spotting the pretty boy's mess of wavy, black hair ten feet away. Chad had Lily pressed against him, one arm snaked around her waist while he waved the other over his head like a douche. My fists clenched reflexively at my sides as I took the last few steps.

"Get off her!" I grabbed Chad's shoulder and yanked him backward.

Lily teetered on five inch heels, lurching forward as she tried to get her balance.

"W-what the hell?" She whipped her head around when I pulled her to me, digging her nails into my forearm.

"Hey, Cameron." Chad looked at me in surprise. "What's up, man?"

"Let me go," Lily slurred, squirming out of my grip and nearly falling on her face.

She swayed in front of me, her confusion deepening as her unfocused eyes squinted at me.

Turning a heated glare to Chad, I stepped forward, towering over him. "Did you give her anything?"

His eyes went wide. "No way. We were just dancing." He lifted his chin indignantly. "I didn't do shit, man. I don't need no roofie to get a chick."

My head snapped at the first flash from the cell phone camera. Several more flashes quickly followed.

Fuck.

Lily crumbled against my side, stumbling as I pushed our way through the tight circle that formed around us, leaving Chad in the center with his mouth hanging open.

"Lemme go." Swiveling her head back to the dance floor, she squirmed in my arms. "I wanna dance some more!"

"Calm down," I growled in her ear, pushing her through the front door.

"You!" Breaking free from me again, she turned, pointing her finger at me. "W-what the fuck is your p-problem?"

Looking down at my shoes when a couple walked past us, I waited for the door to slide shut before I grabbed her wrist. "What is *your* problem?"

Pulling her toward the stairs that led to the taxi stand, I dropped her wrist and nudged her onto the first step. "You're fucking wasted, Lily."

Grabbing the railing, she spun around to face me. "So!" Her face crumbled, her chin trembling as she tried to stay upright. "What do you care?"

Reaching forward, I brushed my thumb over the pale pink lipstick smeared at the corner of her mouth. Her lips were warm and soft. Leaning into my touch, her unfocused eyes drifted to half-mast. My hand slid to the back of her neck, which was damp and cool with sweat.

I pulled her mouth to mine. Her tongue tasted like sweet peppermint as she made a clumsy attempt to drag it from mine when I dove in. Fisting my shirt, she gave in, deepening the kiss until she had to pull away for air. I held her there, my lips hovering an inch from hers.

"I care, Lily."

CHAPTER 15

Reeling back, Lily shoved me with her small fists. "Don't lie to me, Cameron." She held her arms stiff as she swayed in front of me. "I-I came…I came to find you. I begged someone to cover for me at the bar. *Begged*." She snorted, a bubble of wry laughter erupting from her chest. "I'll p-probably lose my job. And your manager t-tells me you b-brought a date." Her knees wobbled, and she dropped to the step, mumbling incoherently.

Kneeling down in front of her, I put my hands on her knees, holding them there while she clumsily tried to push them away.

"Look at me, Lily."

Shaking her head dramatically, she swayed even as she sat.

"Baby, please just look at me."

Her head jerked up, her eyes narrow and unfocused.

"I didn't bring a date. I wasn't here with anyone." I smoothed her hair. "Lindsey didn't tell me you were here. Why didn't you tell me you had to work?"

She looked confused at the question.

"I-I don't know." Shrugging, she hiccupped. "Embarrassed."

Her eyes were softer now, and she stopped trying to push me away. Reaching around her waist, I pulled her up. She giggled, burying her face in my neck.

"Come on, drunk girl." I chuckled. "I'm taking you home."

Clinging to my side, she made it two steps before she whipped her head around.

"I'm going to kick that b-bitch's ass!"

Lifting her off the ground, I pulled her closer.

"Later, baby—let's get out of here."

Kissing her again, I distracted her long enough to get us up the stairs. She didn't need to worry about killing Lindsey. I was going to do that myself. Since Lindsey wasn't human, I doubt anything but a stake to the heart would kill her. So firing her would have to do.

Forgoing the cabstand, I waved down one of the many cabs circling the clubs. I jumped inside and pulled Lily in after me. She threw her leg over mine, nuzzling my neck.

"Baby, give me your address." My eyes nearly rolled to the back of my head when her tongue slid in my ear. "I need to give the cab driver your address."

Before you pass out.

Giggling, she bit down on my earlobe. "Let's have sex," she said in a surprisingly clear and very loud voice.

The cab driver's eyes met mine in the rearview mirror.

"Inside voice, darlin'—give me your address."

"Hm...sixty-six-oh-six Maple...Mapleshade Lane," she huffed. "Now can we have sex?"

Dissolving into a fit of laughs, she pushed her hand under my shirt.

"Did you get that?" I asked the cabbie, trying to keep her hand from going any higher, or God forbid, any lower.

He nodded, turning the volume up on the radio. His gaze continued to drift to the backseat where I was making a lame attempt to fight Lily off. She might have been oblivious to our surroundings, but I was not. It didn't stop my hand from sliding up her skirt to cup her ass.

As the miles passed, Lily's pants became more feverish, her hands more insistent.

"Baby, if you don't stop," I growled, "I will tie you up."

She groaned, digging her fingers into the tender skin on my stomach. Pulling her ear to my mouth, I flicked my tongue over her earlobe. "*And* I won't fuck you."

She quit squirming. Stopped right on the spot. Whatever drunken haze had overtaken her, the threat made it to her foggy brain.

"Patience, baby." I chuckled.

Lily's head popped up when we came to a stop in front of her apartment complex. Reaching in my wallet, I pulled out the fare and a generous tip before grabbing Lily's hand.

"Bye!" she said to the driver, sliding forward on the seat.

Her skirt rode up high enough to give me a nice view of her pale pink panties when she stepped out. Groaning inwardly, I smoothed her skirt before wrapping my arm around her waist and guiding her up the path.

Snuggling into my side as we walked, she tripped over her heels, nearly bringing us both down in a heap. Another fit of laughter overtook her. It was either carry her or risk a broken ankle.

"Please tell me you don't live on the third floor." Crouching over, I looked up at her. "Get on my back. I want to get you there in one piece."

"I can walk!" she protested, swaying in her spot.

"Just do it, Lily."

Standing around and arguing was not nearly as much fun as what I planned to do when I got her inside. She climbed on my back and cinched her legs around my waist. Sticking one hand in the collar of my t-shirt, she scored her nails across my chest and bit my neck. More than a few of her inhibitions were tossed out the window.

"I swear, Lily. I will tie you up if you don't quit." I trudged toward the first group of lights. Telling her I wouldn't fuck her was not only a lie. It was a *damn* lie. It would be a miracle if we made it to her front door and a bigger miracle if we made it to a bed. "Where am I going?"

"Left," she squealed. "Go left."

Pointing at the second door in the alcove, she slid off my

back when I stopped in front of the door. She kicked the mat and dropped to one knee when she spotted the silver glinting under the porch light.

"Why don't you carry your key with you?" Taking the key from her hand, I shoved it in the deadbolt and pushed open the door. "That's dangerous, baby."

"Nah." Waving her hand dismissively, she stumbled over the step on the threshold. "My roommate is always losing her keys."

I stopped in my tracks with one foot inside the door. "You have a roommate?"

A light flicked on in the hallway a few feet away. Lily stepped out of the skirt that was pooled around her ankles.

"Yes, I have a roommate," she mumbled, fumbling with the buttons on her blouse, "but she's not here. She's at her Bob-friend's. I mean, she's at Bobby's, her boyfriend." Exasperated, she tugged the blouse over her head.

Closing the door, I flipped the deadbolt, dropping the key on the table as I closed the gap between us. She stepped back, her eyes going wide when she saw the look on my face. If she thought she could outrun me, she should have considered removing the fuck-me heels first.

My agitation over seeing her with Chad had all but disappeared, but it flamed up deep in my belly when I saw what she had underneath her clothes. A filmy pink bra and matching panties that were so sheer, she might as well have been naked. Grabbing her ass, I pulled her against me, walking us down the hallway.

"Right or left?" I stopped between the two doors at the end of the hall.

Wrapping her legs around my waist, she clamped down on my neck, waving her arm at the door on the left. I would never advocate drinking as a nightly pastime, considering my sordid family history with alcohol, but Lily was the best kind of drunk right now. She was a fucking animal. Biting and grabbing at me wildly.

Crashing through the door, I grabbed her arms, pulling them from my neck when I felt the bed against my shins. I let her fall against the down comforter and bent over to untie the laces on my boots. She grabbed my hair, pulling me forward until I was inches from her center. The heels of her shoes dug in when she arched her back, pushing her hips towards me.

The light from the hallway filtered in, illuminating one-half of her face. She looked like an angel, all tousled, blond hair and creamy skin. And I knew it was me she wanted. Me she wanted against her skin, tasting her.

Dragging her panties down, I pulled them off one leg and spread her open. She gasped when my tongue dipped insider her, the tip making a trail to her clit. I wrapped an arm around her thigh, holding her in place while I circled her in one frenzied motion. She didn't pause when the comforter ripped under the pressure of her spiked heel. She was so wet, so ready, I slid two fingers in. The groan that tore through her was on the verge of a scream.

"Faster...Cam...baby...now."

Riding my hand wildly, she spread her legs to the point I thought her bones would crack. When she started to clench against my fingers, I increased the pace and worked her harder with my tongue.

"Oh, God...oh...God."

Her upper body came off the bed as she rocked against me. She chanted my name until she shuddered, falling against the mattress with a thud. Her fingers slid out of my hair as I pulled away. She followed me with her eyes, and her chest continued to heave as I stripped off my boots and pulled off my shirt. I took out my wallet and grabbed a condom.

"Come here," I said through clenched teeth.

She crawled toward me, her eyes shining fiercely.

"Turn around."

She blinked, rising to her knees.

"Turn. Around." I bit off the words.

Turning, she glanced at me over her shoulder. Then she smiled, her pink tongue darting to the corner of her lip. She was teasing me. Shoving my jeans to my knees, I tore open the foil wrapper with my teeth and slid the condom on without breaking our gaze.

"Take off your bra, baby."

I stroked my cock while she reached behind her and unfastened the bra hooks. I caught it before it fell to the floor.

She shivered when I trailed my hands down her arms to her wrists, positioning them behind her.

"Trust me, baby?" I pulled her to me to whisper in her ear.

She nodded without hesitation, arching into me. Kissing her hair, I gave her a gentle nudge. She fell forward, lying perfectly still. Taking both wrists in one hand, I slipped the shoulder strap of her bra over them and bound her loosely.

Using the head of my cock, I teased her entrance until she writhed. I slid in an inch and felt her tugging me. Pulling me from the inside. With a little more force than I expected, I buried myself so deep there was nothing but her. She owned every sensation in my body as I thrust.

Sliding a hand to her clit when I felt my stomach begin to uncoil, I circled her quickly with just enough pressure to send her crashing to the bottom.

She called my name, begging me to take all of her. And in that moment, when I clung to her, spilling my release, she stole a piece of me that I could never get back. Or I gave it willingly. Either way, something shifted, and I felt it so intensely I didn't know whether to run or hold her so tight she could never get away.

CHAPTER 16

Light poured through the shades of the unfamiliar room as I woke. Propping myself up on my elbows, I took in the surroundings.

Lily's room. I would recognize the scent anywhere, even if all the drawings on the wall didn't give it away.

A small desk sat in the corner of the cramped space. Books were strewn on the surface and on the floor beneath. Next to the desk was an easel with a white sheet of drawing paper clipped to the top, the chair in front of it facing the bed. I scrubbed a hand down my face and scratched my stubbly jaw. I needed a strong cup of coffee and a toothbrush. And Lily. Sitting up, I threw my legs over the side of the bed and stepped into my jeans, pulling up the zipper without buttoning them.

Walking over to the single brew coffee pot on the desk, I looked around for the pods, and spotted the still steaming cup of coffee next to the easel. I took a sip. Strong and sweet. My favorite.

Dropping into the chair, I stared at the half finished sketch. A male image, with well-defined muscles, sleeping on his side. Strands of long hair fell over the face. *My face.* The parted lips. The nose. Even the brows. They were all perfect. Exactly how I would imagine I looked when I slept.

"What are you going to do?" a muffled female voice asked beyond the door.

"I don't know...I'm...Oh, God. I don't know."

It was Lily. And she was crying. I jumped out of my seat, moving to the door. My hand was poised on the knob when a phone rang.

"It's my mom," Lily breathed. "Should I answer?"

"You've got to answer, sweetie," the female voice sighed. "She won't give up."

"H-hello. Hi, M-mom. No—yes, it's me." She sniffed. Another voice rang in the room, fainter. Lily must have put the phone on speaker.

"...how embarrassed we are. What are you thinking? You're Marcus Tennison's daughter. You looked like a common slut." The woman seethed with bitterness. "Do you know your father's office has already fielded a dozen phone calls? Craig is beside himself. Don't you ever think about what you're doing, Lily?" The woman barely took a breath, winding up her tirade. "It's one thing having a daughter that's an artist. That alone is enough to ensure that any decent men won't be asking you out. Now you're acting like a groupie."

A groupie.

"I-I wasn't acting like a g-groupie, Mother." Lily's agitation heightened. "C-Cam—my friend invited me to watch his b-band practice. There were ph-photographers there. I—"

"Enough, Lily." The woman cut her off. "Don't lie to me. There are pictures online of you in a club. Your friend was holding you up. You looked drunk, Lily. Or high. We let you pursue this pipe dream. We haven't interfered—"

"Interfered?" Lily nearly choked on the word. "Y-you k-kicked me out! You took my c-car, and I have been w-working two jobs to pay for school. Why? B-because I didn't apply for a scholarship. Who would believe that a T-Tennison would need help with tuition? You d-don't pay my bills, Mother. You or Daddy. I don't n-need to ask p-permission to date someone."

"Date? My dear, that man is not dating you."

"You're right, Mother," Lily said, coolly. "He's f-fucking me. Maybe if you t-tried *that* sometime, D-Daddy wouldn't be bang-ng M-Marcia."

"Lillian Rochelle Tennison! How dare—"

Pulling the door open when I heard the loud crash, I saw Lily sitting with her head in her hands, slumped in the hallway. She was wearing the t-shirt I had on last night, and her hair was knotted on top of her head in a messy bun. Her friend stood frozen, looking from Lily to me.

"I'm Tessa, Lily's roommate."

"Cameron." I smiled tightly.

"I'll leave you two alone..."

I nodded when Tessa looked at me imploringly. It was obvious she cared about Lily. I could see it in our silent exchange. *Don't hurt her.* The words were as clear as if she spoke them aloud.

Tessa walked quietly to where Lily's cell phone was smashed to pieces, kneeling down to pick them up before she disappeared into the room across the hall.

Lily looked up at me, mascara running down her cheeks. Her chin trembled.

"Cameron...I..." Her face contorted, and she looked away.

Stepping to her cautiously, I crouched down and brushed the hair off her face. A copy of the Dallas Morning News was folded at her side, turned to the society page. Right there in black and white was a picture of us wading through the photographers at the stadium yesterday.

Is Cameron Knight playing a new tune? Caged guitarist spotted getting cozy with Lillian Tennison, socialite daughter of high profile business magnate Marcus Tennison, in Arlington.

Scooping her up, I carried her to her room. She curled into a ball with her back to me when I laid her on the bed. I was so wrapped up in my own head, I never thought about what Lily might be risking by getting involved with me. She plunged in, stepped into my world. With no promise of anything more than a few days that I assumed she would be grateful to have.

Her shoulders quaked softly as she wept. Something stronger than my fear of my own frailties gripped me. The mattress dipped as I crawled next to her, wrapping myself around her until I felt her grow still.

"I'm sorry, Lily."

She turned in my arms, so close our noses were an inch apart.

"W-why?" Her brow furrowed in confusion. "I'm not. Well, except for last n-night."

Breaking our gaze, she looked down, running her finger back and forth between my collarbone and the hollow of my neck.

"I don't know w-what I was thinking," she muttered, "show-ing up like that. L-letting that stupid bitch get to me." Looking up, the tears welled in her eyes, and she blinked furiously to keep them at bay. "T-thank you for taking me home. You didn't have to."

"Darlin', of course I took you home. I asked you to go with me."

"I wanted to, but I couldn't miss work. I got someone to cover for me, and I jumped into a cab. When Lindsey said that you didn't want to see me, that you were there with s-someone else, I figured you were probably still mad." A tear rolled down her cheek.

"Baby, I wasn't mad." Brushing the tear away with the pad of my thumb, I kissed her wet cheek. "I was hurt. And I said something stupid."

"No—" She shook her head, bumping our noses.

"Yeah, I did." Cutting her off, I slid my hand to the back of her neck, pressing my forehead to hers so that I could look in her eyes. "And I'm sorry. But I didn't know you were at the club. I would never send you away. I was fucking miserable before you showed up."

Rolling over with her under me, I watched another tear slide out of the corner of her eye and disappear into her hair.

"Lily, I don't know how to do...*this*." Kissing her cheek, the salt on my lips added to the tension thrumming through me. "I don't want to hurt you. But, shit—I want to be with you. However. Wherever. Can we try?"

Moving her mouth to mine, she searched out my tongue with hers. I didn't know whether she was agreeing or silencing me without words. Either way, she didn't say no. I would take that…for now.

CHAPTER 17

I'd only worn a tuxedo once. And that was a rental. I opted to buy this one. I wanted to show Lily that I was serious about stepping into her world. Taking her to the ballet or art galleries. Every place. Any place.

I looked down at the guy with the tape measure hanging around his neck. He was crawling between my legs. Tucking. Pinning. Groping.

I swear he was groping.

Lily finally returned with a black zippered bag draped over her arm. Stifling a laugh, she settled into the chair in the sitting room to witness the spectacle.

"Not funny," I mouthed when the guy made the second pass over my package, smoothing down the front of the slacks.

Lily pursed her lips, trying to keep the lilt of laughter from her voice.

"Mr. Gravis, can you have this delivered to The Mansion before five o'clock?"

Turning to her, a smile lit his chubby face while he continued to work me over.

"Of course, Lily." Standing, he walked to her side, cocking his head to survey me. "The jacket—it is a perfect fit. A little tuck in the trousers." He waved his arms through the air in a sweeping gesture. "Voila!"

Looking at Lily like I wasn't there, he cocked a brow. "A perfect body for the clothes, no?"

Lily's gaze swept over me. Our eyes locked, and a pink flush crept into her cheeks.

"Yes. He is perfect."

Mr. Gravis nodded and gratefully—*thankfully*—departed so I could change. Lily crossed the room, kneeling in front of me. My hand went to her hair.

"Don't get any ideas." Looking up, she narrowed her eyes. "You're full of pins. You'll be lucky if your balls make it out unscathed."

Sliding the trousers off my hips, she slapped my leg.

"Cameron—step back." She shook her head, looking up at me again. "Too much time on the road, buddy. I'm not blowing you in the dressing room at Saks."

Scampering to her feet, she glided across the dressing room, clipping the trousers on a hanger. I came up behind her, flexing my hips so she could see what she was missing. When my hand found its way under her shirt, I realized it was me that was missing out. As she wiggled her butt, the seam of her jeans grazed the head of my cock through my boxer briefs.

"Later, you sex fiend," she teased, slipping out of my grasp.

"I see how it is." I crossed the room and pulled on my jeans, carefully tucking my erection inside. "Now that you're my girlfriend, all the fun stuff is going to stop. No more limo sex. No more tying you up with your pretty pink bra."

Her hand was poised above the black garment bag that held her dress. Her pouty lips turned down in the reflection of the dressing room mirror.

"Don't tease me, Cameron," she said softly. "It's not funny."

If she thought I was teasing, she was dead wrong. I was terrified. And very serious. Moving the few steps until I was at her back, I slid my arms around her waist.

"I'm not teasing you, darlin'." Holding her gaze in the mirror, I nuzzled her ear. "Before you get all starry eyed, you should know I haven't had a girlfriend since the eleventh grade. So I probably suck at it."

She turned in my arms, the blue of her eyes quieting my every doubt. But her frown remained.

"Try not to hurt me, Cam." Laying a hand over my heart, she kissed me softly. "Please try."

CHAPTER 18

I paced the length of the suite while Dave set up the special dinner I had ordered. The stiff collar of the starched white shirt chaffed my neck. Running a finger between the fabric and my skin, I ignored the feeling of being choked by my own formal-wear.

"You look very nice, Cameron." Dave reached in his pocket for a lighter.

Two tapered candles sat in the center of the small table, with a centerpiece of fresh lilies between them. Looking down at the flowers then up to Dave's searching gaze, I smiled.

"Thanks, Dave."

He lit the candles and straightened the dinnerware, the linens, and finally the centerpiece. "We sure are going to miss Lily around here," he mused. "She was a joy to work with. Such a special girl."

Stopping in my tracks, I stared at Dave with a blank expression. "Why would you miss Lily? She's…" *In the next room.*

After we'd returned from the mall, I had drawn her a bath and slid in behind her, helping her program the new cell phone she bought. The bath and the sex we had in the tub were her concession for not allowing me to *buy* her the damn phone. She finally chased me out so she could get ready for our date.

Dave didn't meet my gaze, checking the flame under the chaffing dishes. "Mr. Greg let her go this afternoon. It seems that she was in the papers today. The Mansion does quite a bit of business with the Tennison Foundation. I was under the impression that it was not Mr. Greg's choice." He finally looked at me, his eyes serious and troubled. "Still, I was hoping that someone would have the balls to stand up for her."

Swallowing hard, I sunk into the uncomfortable Louis XIV chair. Fired. Because of me.

"Are you sure?"

Nodding, his expression turned sympathetic. "I take it you were unaware."

"Hell no, I wasn't aware." I pointed to the closed bedroom door. "Is *she* aware?"

His eyes widened. "Miss Lily is here?"

"Of course she is." I cocked my head, blinking at him. "You thought *this* was for someone else?"

Dave turned almost as crimson as the roses I had delivered for Lily prior to our arrival. Four dozen American Beauties in elaborate crystal vases. One dozen for each of the days we spent together.

"It's not my place to judge," he said quietly. "I didn't mean to offend."

"It's fine, Dave." Trying to mask my irritation, I walked over and patted him on the shoulder. "Do me a favor. Don't tell anyone Lily is here. She should be out any minute. I can take things from here."

He nodded, taking a final inventory of the table.

"Of course. Have a pleasant evening, Cameron."

Giving me a tight smile, he turned and headed for the door.

I pulled out my phone, tapping Chase's name to open the text box. My fingers hovered over the keypad. I'd always turned to my brother for advice. Guidance. I hit the button on the side, and the screen went dark.

Not this time.

The knob on the double door to the bedroom turned, and

Lily poked her head out.

"I heard the front door close," she said playfully. "Is the coast clear?"

I slipped the phone into my front pocket. "All clear, darlin'."

She stepped into the room, the slit on the side of the deep burgundy dress falling open to reveal an expanse of her creamy thigh as she sashayed toward me. The dress was strapless, with just a hint of soft skin spilling over the top of the bodice. Her blond hair was gathered in a loose bun with a few strands falling on her shoulders.

"You like?" She twirled in front of me.

Her smile faded when she looked at me, rooted to my spot.

"I-I really liked the color." She flushed. "If it's too much—"

"Baby, you're beautiful." Stepping forward, I took her hands, looking in her eyes as I brought them to my lips. "Stunning."

She smiled. A brilliant smile, shy and full of promise.

Try not to hurt me, Cam. Please try.

I lowered my mouth to hers for one quick taste.

"Dinner's ready," I murmured against her lips. "Unless you'd like to have dessert first." Running my hand over her hip, I groaned. "Please tell me you're wearing something underneath this dress."

Pecking my lips, she pulled me toward the table.

"I'll never tell." Sinking into the chair, she crossed her legs and let the slit fall open. It stopped just short of the Promised Land. "You'll have to find out for yourself. Later."

My gaze was fixed at the top of her thigh. She grabbed my hand when I reached for her, seemingly unable to stop myself. Bringing my fingers to her lips, she gave me a wicked grin and slid her pink tongue over the tip of my index finger.

Later.

CHAPTER 19

"Would you like another glass of wine, baby?" I leaned close to Lily's ear, running my hand over the curve of her hip as we waited in the theater lobby. She'd kept me at bay, even scooting over to the far end of the seat in the limo when my fingers moved up the slit on her dress.

She looked at the line at the bar and up at the clock above the huge doors to the inner theater.

"One more." She drained her glass, and she handed it to me. The smile on her face was plastered in place. We stood off to the side of the bustling crowd as she surveyed the room with a series of sidelong glances.

"I'll be right back."

She yipped when I leaned in for a kiss and squeezed her ass before I sauntered off. Lily may have been nervous as hell, for whatever reason, but I was relaxed. I caught a few stares, but quickly realized it was from my long hair, not because someone recognized me.

It wasn't that I was recognized everywhere I went. It was when an overzealous fan crossed the line that things got awkward. Having a random chick pull out her tit and insist I sign it was surreal enough; doing it in front of my mother was downright embarrassing. I'd yet to see how Lily would react, but not bringing it into her world was a relief.

Grabbing the two glasses of wine, I looked around for Lily. I dismissed the small group of six or seven that were standing to my right, until I saw the burgundy of her dress when someone moved to the outside of the group. Her gaze fell on mine, panic written all over her face.

Marching up, I cleared my throat. "Excuse me."

Several sets of eyes turned to me as I stepped inside the tight circle.

"Here you go, darlin'." Handing Lily her glass, I dropped my hand to her waist and pulled her to my side.

Every muscle in her body was tense.

"Cameron, I'd like you to m-meet my p-parents." She motioned at the couple in front of us. "M-Marcus and A-Abigail T-Tennison."

"Lillian," her mother admonished, without acknowledging me. "All those speech classes, and you still stutter."

The guy at her father's side chuckled. "Sometimes it was kind of cute," he said, eyeing her over the top of his wine glass. "Not always, though, eh, Lily?"

"Mr. Tennison." Extending my hand to her father, I kept my gaze on the asshole at his side that hadn't taken his eyes off my girl. "Cameron Noble."

Marcus Tennison had the same piercing blue eyes, the same high cheekbones as his daughter. He was a formidable man, but at the moment, his gaze was soft. Wistful. He hadn't taken his eyes off Lily. "Mr. Noble." Turning his attention to me, he squeezed my hand firmly. "My wife, Abigail."

Her father gave cursory introductions to the other two couples while Lily stood awkwardly, sipping her wine.

"And this is Craig." Marcus awkwardly patted the guy on the back. "He's works at the Tennison Foundation."

Craig. The ex-fiancé. The loser that dumped Lily for dropping out of business school.

"I thought your name was Knight. That's what the papers said. Aren't you a part of that rock band?" Craig glanced over me with disdain.

"Knight is my stage name."

His gaze dropped to my arm that was wrapped around Lily. "But you can call me Mr. Noble if you'd like."

He startled at the petite blond that slipped in beside him. She leaned up and kissed him on the cheek before turning to the group and flashing a million dollar smile. The best smile that modern dentistry could buy. It died on her lips when her eyes locked on Lily.

"Lily—it's nice to see you again." Moving closer to Craig, she forced the corners of her mouth to bend. "I didn't think you attended the ballet. Anymore at least."

"H-hello, A-Amber." Taking a deep breath, Lily seemed to search for the next word. "I-I…" Giving up, she snapped her mouth shut, taking another sip of her wine. Amber turned to me, her eyes going wide the second recognition dawned. A flush of color started at her collar and worked its way to her cheeks.

"Oh…my," she breathed. "You're Cameron. Cameron Knight."

Hitching a brow at Craig, I gave her a tight smile. "That I am."

"You're here…at the ballet." Amber seemed confused. "With Lily?"

Craig snorted, taking another gulp of wine.

All eyes were on me. Except Lily's. She stared at the floor, her mouth set in a frown. "I've never been to the ballet. But since my girlfriend is such a huge supporter, I figured I might as well get used to taking her," I said, shifting my gaze to Craig. "I wouldn't want anybody to accuse me of not appreciating the arts."

Nodding slowly, Marcus was on the verge of a smile when Amber spoke.

"How long have you two been…*dating*?" The jab was directed at Lily, but Amber looked at me innocently.

Lily stiffened to the point of shattering beneath my touch. My fingers tightened on her hip as I felt the first syllable struggling to escape her throat.

"Long enough to know I'm a lucky guy." Ignoring the rest of the group, I let my gaze settle on Abigail. "I've never met anyone as special as your daughter, Mrs. Tennison. I can't imagine how proud you must be of her."

Lily looked at her mother, waiting for the tiniest scrap of kindness. She leaned forward, as if she could pull it from her mother.

"Quite," Abigail said, her cold gaze never leaving mine. When the lights flickered, she slipped her hand in the crook of her husband's arm. "If you'll excuse us, the ballet is about to begin."

Marcus leaned in, brushing Lily's cheek with a soft kiss. "Have a good night, Lily Bear," he murmured, before pulling away.

Looking solely at Lily, I almost didn't notice his outstretched hand. I shook it mechanically, mumbling my goodbye.

"Goodnight, D-Daddy." Lily shifted her gaze to Abigail. "Goodnight, M-Mom; it w-was n-nice to—" Her face fell when her mother turned away without letting her finish.

Fusing her lips tight, Lily nodded her goodbyes to the other two couples, her eyes never leaving her mother's back as the woman walked away. Shuddering, Lily shrank into me when the doors shut behind them.

"So, Lily…" Smelling blood in the water, Craig leaned in to deliver the final blow. "Have you sold any paintings, or are you planning on keeping your career in food and beverage?"

His derisive laughter snapped Lily out of her haze. Stepping forward, her blue eyes ignited with fury.

"Don't think that just b-because you have my f-father fooled that I don't know exactly who you are. I know w-what you did—calling my boss." She turned to Amber, whose chin had dropped. "I thought you were my f-friend, Amber. But you two deserve each other. And just so you know, when Craig gets d-drunk, he still calls *me*."

Snapping her mouth shut, Amber turned a stony gaze on Craig before her mask of serenity returned. "That's pathetic, Lily. Almost as pathetic as dragging your one night stand to the ballet and trying to pass him off as your boyfriend." She lifted her chin. "Clearly you've been sniffing too many paint fumes."

I slipped my arm around Lily's waist. "I think it's about time you two go find your seats. Or better yet—" Pulling our tickets from the pocket of my jacket, I shoved them at Craig. "Take ours. I'm sure they're better. I don't think I could stand sitting in the same room with y'all, and I sure as hell don't want my girl anywhere near you." Shifting my gaze to Amber, I looked her up and down before turning back to Craig. "Lily's a brilliant artist. So I'd think twice before putting her down, because one day she'll be able to buy and sell your ass. And probably mine. But that's okay, because I'll be there when she does it."

Looking up at me in disbelief, Lily's mouth hung open. The only thing I wanted more than to put Craig in the hospital was getting her alone so I could make her believe every word I'd said.

Pulling her to my side, I looked down at her and raised a brow. "What do you say, baby? Let's get out of here. I think we've had enough culture for one night."

Lily smiled. That heart-stopping smile that was only for me. Turning toward the door, I stopped when Craig's hand came down hard on my shoulder.

"You want to step outside, fucker?" he bit out, the fabric of my coat twisting out of his grasp when I spun around.

"You've been watching too many movies, son," I growled, yanking at the tie around my neck. "But in this version, you don't get to walk away with your teeth. I'll be happy to save you the trip outside and drop you right here."

I felt Lily's hand on my back, a second before I heard her heels clicking on the marble floor as she walked away. Glancing over my shoulder, I closed my eyes and prayed for self-control. The rush of wind when she pushed open the door blew her hair. Swaths of golden strands were the last thing I saw before the glass door whooshed shut behind her.

The girl made me forget about all the things that were important to me. Or what I used to think was important. Letting some chump off the hook to chase a girl? Not in this lifetime.

Cursing, I turned on my heel and took a few steps, Craig's

insults rising up behind me.

"Just remember, I got there first." he jeered. "'Course, I wouldn't touch her now. If she let you hit it, who knows how many other guys have had a go at her."

That's the ticket. He found the one spot on my soft underbelly that penetrated my armor.

My fist was already cocked when I spun and met the piercing, blue eyes of Marcus Tennison, standing two feet behind Craig. His facial features were not the only thing he shared with his daughter. The crease on his brow, deepened by age, showed the measure of his displeasure at the moment.

Dropping my hand to my side, I stared blankly at Craig.

"What's the matter, chickenshit?" Craig took a step forward. "Cat got your tongue?"

Fuck it. Even the great Marcus Tennison wasn't going to keep me from pounding this motherfucker into next week. Lunging, Marcus beat me to it, yanking Craig backward and out of my reach.

Whipping his head around in surprise, Craig deflated the moment he realized who had hold of his collar. Amber's mouth fell open, her eyes as wide as saucers.

"Marcus—"

"Shut up, Craig," Marcus spat, turning his attention to me. "Cameron, if you wouldn't mind finding my daughter, I'll handle this matter for you." He gave Craig a sidelong glance, the disdain evident. "I had my chance to play the hero. Sadly, I didn't. Don't tell Lily I intervened. It's an empty gesture, at best. But rest assured, I will deal with this." Craig winced when Marcus gave him a firm shake. "I love my daughter, and I want her to be happy. If you can make her happy, please do. She deserves it." He gave me the shadow of a smile. "If you'll excuse me."

"Yes, sir."

Craig met my gaze briefly before Marcus turned him in the direction of the theatre, his hand still firmly on the collar of the younger man's jacket. Amber stood frozen, looking over her shoulder at the asshat being dragged through the lobby like a whipped dog.

I couldn't resist one parting shot. When I stepped in front of her, she swiveled her head to me, shock painting every feature on her face.

"Looks like you bet on the wrong horse." I looked her up and down, unable to disguise my contempt. "I was more than willing to put your boy in the hospital, but I think Marcus has that handled." I barked out a laugh. "And we both know Craig is the only one that has a problem with his tongue. Mine works just fine."

The flush that crept into her cheeks rivaled the color of Lily's burgundy dress. I didn't bother waiting around to see if she burst into flames because of it.

Turning on my heel, I jogged for the door, scanning the area in front of the building when I stepped outside. Lily was seated on a stone bench under a tree, her gaze firmly planted on the ground. Her head snapped up when she heard my footsteps approaching.

"C-Cameron." Jumping up, she flung herself into my arms. "W-what happened? Please tell me you didn't hit him."

I cringed. Hitting Craig was exactly what I had intended to do. From Lily's reaction, she wasn't down with the plan.

"Lily—"

"We've got to get out of here." Pulling away, she grabbed my hand, dragging me toward the area where the limos where parked. "He's going to call the police. He's a fucking coward. You could go to jail."

She turned to me when I stopped, her eyes wide with panic.

"C-Cameron, please, we have to go." Tugging my arm again, her brow knit in consternation when I wouldn't budge.

"I didn't hit him, baby." Seeing the relief that swept over her, I wrapped her in my arms. "I just talked to him. We came to an understanding. He keeps your name out of his mouth, and he gets to keep his teeth."

It was a dick move. Marcus was the real hero, but I was taking the credit. I'd have to tell her what happened. Eventually. Right now, I needed all the help I could get.

"Thank God." Sliding her hands underneath my jacket, she

fisted my shirt, holding me tight. "I couldn't handle it if you went to jail. B-because of me."

"It wouldn't be the first time."

That had sounded better in my head. Lily was not the kind of girl to be impressed with my brawling skills.

"Well," she said, lifting her face to me and pressing a kiss to my neck, "I'm glad I was the girl that got the benefit of your gallant behavior tonight."

Girl? I barked out a laugh. "Darlin', I've never gotten in a fight over a girl." Cupping her neck, I ran my thumb over her jaw. "I've only put the hurt on someone when they were fucking with someone I cared about. Logan and the guys, my brother…" I kissed her nose. "But never a chick. Although, I don't think I'd be able to control myself if someone ever tried to hurt you. Luckily, I make enough money to hire a really good attorney."

She melted in my arms, holding me so tight I could feel the rise and fall of her chest with every breath she took.

"Come on, baby." Turning us toward the parking lot, I pulled her to my side. "I'm tired. And I'm dying to find out what you got hiding under that dress."

CHAPTER 20

Lily was sprawled on her stomach, the sheets tangled around her as she slept. Her burgundy dress was crumpled next to the bed. The little firecracker actually took me to the Dallas Ballet wearing nothing but that dress and a pair of heels. She was perfect for me in every way. So perfect, the thought of leaving after the show tomorrow tore a hole in my gut.

Stirring when I ran my hand over her ass, she turned over, her eyes fluttering open for a second before they drifted shut.

My fingers danced over her stomach, coming to rest on her breast. Her nipple pebbled under my touch, and her legs fell open. Yeah, she was perfect.

Snuggling next to her, I continued to explore her body. Soft hips. Delicate wrists. Taut stomach.

"What are you doing?" she said with a yawn.

"Looking at you."

"Like what you see?"

"I love what I see."

My breath hitched, and my heart skipped a beat. Labels. Commitments. Complications. I had gotten past the complications. And even the commitment. Lily was mine. Whatever that meant. But I'd never been in love. I wasn't about to ruin this by slapping a useless label on it. Even though I wanted her—needed her—as much as my next breath.

"Come to Austin with me." I didn't look up, continuing to trace my finger across her stomach.

I L-O-V-E Y-O-U. Testing it out, I drew the letters on her stomach. My head snapped up when she giggled.

"That tickles."

I ran my palm over her smooth skin, like I was erasing a chalkboard.

"What do you say, baby. Come to Austin with me?"

Rolling on my back, I grabbed her hand and stared at the predawn light that peaked through the curtains.

"I can't." She sighed. "I have to finish school. I'm done in May."

"What happens then?"

"I don't know," she said softly.

"What do you mean, darlin'?"

Silence. Deafening silence.

"Come here." I tugged her hand. "Talk to me."

More silence. Lily hadn't opened up to me about losing her job at The Mansion. Not yet. Mild discomfort crept into my chest as something tightened around my neck. The lump that formed in my throat was enough to choke me. She finally turned, draping herself across my chest.

"My mother is on the board of the Fine Arts League. They run the fundraisers for all the museums. Coordinate all the events." A tear splashed on my chest. "I haven't had any response to any of the letters I sent. Even from the small galleries. I finally sent some resumes out to other cities."

"Do you think your mother would do that?" I stroked her hair, knowing the answer. I saw the look on the woman's face last night. The contempt. "Why, Lily?"

"To prove a point, I guess. I didn't follow the plan." She sighed deeply, nuzzling her face into my neck. "It was all set. They wanted me to marry Craig, even though I didn't love him. Even though he was cheating on me with Amber. I guess they thought, with my speech problem, I was lucky that he paid me any attention at all."

Her speech was not a problem. Not to me. It was a part of her, like her expressive brow and the sky blue depths of her eyes. It was beautiful.

Lifting her chin, I bent to kiss her lips.

"Maybe the words don't come because they don't want to leave these beautiful lips any more than I do." Pulling her forward, I bent to kiss her throat. "If I could live here—*right here*—I would."

She looked down at me. Like she didn't believe me. Like she couldn't.

"My parents don't see it that way. They kicked me out, and my dad hired Craig." She sniffed, her chin quivering with defiance. "They took my car and left me without a penny. I rode the bus until I saved enough money waitressing to buy a car. I slept on Tessa's couch until I could afford to pitch in for rent, and we got a two bedroom. Now I'm graduating, and Tessa wants to move in with her boyfriend. I talked to the manager at the bar. I can pick up enough shifts to swing a one bedroom until someone hires me at a gallery."

Lily was strong. As strong as anyone I'd ever met. She'd done what few people could. She'd had it all, and she walked away. Rather than sell her soul.

"Come to Austin." Running my hands to her hips, I folded her in my arms. Protecting her. I would always protect her. "After you graduate. Lily, I want to be with you."

"I can't let you support me." She dropped her forehead to my chest. "We barely know each other. I want to be with you… please believe me."

"I do." Resting my chin on the top of her head, I tightened my grip. "But I wouldn't be supporting you, baby. Just taking care of things until you find something in Austin. I want us to be together; I don't care what it takes."

Sliding under my arm, she scooted to the side of the bed and felt around on the floor. She crawling back to me and hiked her leg over mine, straddling me. She bent down and kissed my stomach, working her way up to my chest, my neck, and finally my mouth. Fumbling around for my hand, she pressed the foil packet in my palm.

She pressed her forehead to mine, her sweet honey taste lingering on my lips. Blue eyes, clouded with sorrow, looked deep into mine. Pressing a kiss to my bottom lip, her eyes drifted shut.

"Love me, Cameron."

Turning her over, I ripped open the packet and rolled the condom on, settling on top of her. I slid inside and surrendered. She asked me to love her. And I did.

"Wake up."

Lily pressed a kiss to my brow and placed a cup of coffee on the nightstand. Reaching inside the pocket of the oversized robe that The Mansion provided, she handed me my phone.

"This thing has been vibrating nonstop. They're going to send a search party if you don't answer your calls."

Throwing it on the bed, I reached inside the robe, warming my hands on her silky skin.

"What time is it?"

"Nine thirty." She sat on the edge of the bed. "Do you have rehearsal today?"

Groaning, I threw an arm over my forehead.

"This afternoon." I peeked at her. "Go with me?"

She chuckled. "Talk to Logan first. See what's going on. I'm not going to be the Yoko Ono to your John Lennon."

"Hm. Beatles references. You're getting the hang of this quick. You'll make a perfect rock star girlfriend. All you need is a few miniskirts and some knee-high boots." Sitting up, I grabbed the coffee. "I'm buying."

"I have enough people trying to buy me, Cameron," she said quietly. "I don't need anything from you."

Standing, she reached for her tote bag and headed for the bathroom. "I'm grabbing a shower."

I threw my legs over the side of the bed. She glanced at me over her shoulder.

"Alone," she said.

Dropping the robe, she shook her ass, scampering into the bathroom when I jumped off the bed and gave chase. The lock clicked into place before I could reach her.

"Not fair." I slapped the door. "Tease!"

Smiling, I sauntered over to the nightstand and snagged the coffee. I felt around until I found my phone and walked into the living room. Lily had ordered breakfast. Piling a plate with fruit and a couple of pastries, I walked over to the desk and sank into the chair, flipping through the long list of texts. I tapped out a message to Logan, assuring him I would be at rehearsal. Deleting all of Lindsey's texts, I took a bite of the pastry and wiped my hands.

Bringing up the email program on my computer, I typed a long message to Chase. I chewed my lip, trying to find the right words. I started and stopped, rewriting it several times. After reading it over, I shrugged and hit the send button.

The email program disappeared, leaving only a web page open. An email from Lily's mother, time stamped this morning at 5:42 a.m. Lily must have used my computer to check her account when she woke up.

Don't look.

My cursor hovered above the small "X" in the corner. After peeking at the bathroom door, I opened the email. Scanning the first paragraph, my chest constricted and my fists clenched with rage.

Lillian,

After the spectacle you made of yourself at the ballet, it has become apparent that your father and I have made some grave mistakes. Your dalliance with that musician is nothing more than a cry for help. Help that we are prepared to offer.

I would be remiss if I did not point out that I feel you have chosen a career path that is an utter waste of time and completely without merit. As you know, I am a supporter of the arts. After all, it was I who sought out the art-centered therapy to help you with your handicap when you were just a child. I couldn't help but notice during our brief interaction that your speech impediment is more pronounced than ever. Are you taking steps to rectify the situation, Lillian, or have you chosen to embrace your disability and give up?

As I understand it, there is $24,800 that is due and payable before you will be eligible to graduate. It is unfortunate that your indiscretion with your musician friend cost you your job at The Mansion. Their $10,000 employee contribution would have gone a long way toward reducing your debt at the university. I dare say that your job as a barmaid will not go far in helping you meet your goal.

Your father and I have generously agreed to wipe this debt from your record. In addition, we will purchase a car for your graduation as a gesture of good will. As the recently appointed chair of the Fine Arts League, I will use all my resources to persuade the museum or gallery of your choice to hire you. From what I understand, you have been unsuccessful at securing a job in your field, such as it is.

As for the terms, they are simple. You will move back home, enter an intensive program for your speech impediment, and above all, you will cease all contact with Cameron Noble. You know, as well as I, that he will do nothing more than use you, possibly passing you off to one of his friends when he is through.

I await your response. You will come to realize that you don't have many choices in the matter.

As I slumped in the chair in disbelief, the rage gave way to pain. For Lily. Her mother still didn't see who she was. Her strength, her talent, or her grace. Abigail was taking away all of Lily's options. Or so she thought.

Slamming the computer shut when I heard the bathroom door creak open, I picked up my phone, opening the text from Chase.

Of course, I'll speak with Tanner. I'm sure he would agree to look at a sample of her work. As for the rest of it, I can only tell you to follow your gut, little brother. You're nothing like Dad. The only way that you can hurt this girl is if you choose to. I'll see you Sunday. Love you, bro.

Breathing a sigh of relief, I tapped in a response.

I'll call you after rehearsal. Things are more complicated than I thought. I'll work it out. Thanks for your help. Have the barbecue ready and the beer on ice. See you Sunday.

Lily walked into the living room, her damp hair falling in waves around her shoulders. She walked over and kissed the top of my head.

"I've got a few hours to kill before rehearsal." Twisting the sash of her robe around my hand, I looked up at her. "What do you want to do today, baby?"

Pushing the hair out of my face, she smiled. It didn't reach her eyes. For the first time I looked at the crease on her forehead, the perfect imperfection where all her worry and all her doubts were etched, and I wished it wasn't there.

"I don't care what we do." The crease deepened, even as her smile grew. "As long as we do it together."

CHAPTER 21

While waiting for Logan in the lobby, I slumped against a pillar with my arms folded over my chest. Lily was asleep on the sectional when I left, curled up under a blanket. I sat for an hour, maybe more, just watching her.

And then it came. The words for a song, bitter and sweet, poured out of me. Straight from my gut. The rush, the feeling of perfection that I'd only known on stage, was there. In the quiet of that room with no bass, no drums, no instrument to accompany me. Just her soft breath.

I was so gone for this girl, tearing myself away, even to do the thing I was born to do, was hard.

Logan sauntered into the lobby, sunglasses firmly affixed, with Greg on his heels. Greg had his reasons for firing Lily. The same pressures we were under from the label that forced us to do asinine things we didn't agree with. A week ago it wouldn't have mattered. If I banged a waitress, and she lost her job, that was the price. For her.

Cringing at the thought and the selfish motivation behind it, I put my head down. I couldn't *not* say something to Greg if he walked up to me. The problem is what I would say.

"Ready to roll?" Logan said, stepping in front of me.

Nodding, I turned for the door.

"Cameron, can I talk to you for a second?" Greg said solemnly.

"Not a good time."

Logan gave me a sidelong glance, matching my brisk pace as we walked.

"It's about Lily."

Turning, I stalked toward him. "What do you want to say Greg?" I barked. "That you sacrificed her to please a client? She was counting on this job." Shaking my head, I glared at him. "Did you ever wonder why some asshole at the Tennison Foundation was so interested in getting her canned? It's her father's company, for Christ's sake. Even a moron could figure out there was an ulterior motive."

Greg shifted his gaze to Logan, who stood at my back, his arms folded over his chest. He didn't know the details. Not yet. But Logan had my back. Always.

"We have rules, Cameron." He shook his head, looking down at his shoe. "She broke them. I like Lily—"

"Like her?" I snorted. "You were practically humping her leg in the lounge the other night. You wanted to take her to my show and who knows what else. How many rules did that break?"

He snapped his mouth shut, and the righteous indignation left his posture.

"That's what I thought." I leaned forward, and he flinched. "Dick move, dude. Keep my girl's name out of your mouth, and if you see her—walk away."

Turning on my heel, I marched toward the door, slamming my palm against the glass to push it open. Sliding into the waiting limo, I yanked off my baseball cap and raked a hand through my hair.

"You want to tell me what that was about?" Ducking into the limo, Logan sat on the opposite seat, stretching his legs in front of him.

Shaking my head, I leaned forward, resting my arms on my knees.

"Lily's father," I grumbled. "He runs the Tennison Foundation. Shit, he is the Tennison Foundation. He had her fired over the pictures in the paper."

"Marcus Tennison?" Logan whistled when I nodded. "That dude is major. I'm glad I didn't fuck his daughter."

Lurching forward, I wanted to throttle him, but I kept my seat. "I didn't fuck her!"

Arching a brow, he draped an arm over the back of the seat. "You didn't fuck her?"

"I didn't *just* fuck her." Slumping into the seat, I let my head fall back against the soft leather. Logan knew everything about me. The good, the bad, and the very ugly. "I have feelings for her. I want to take her back to Austin. See where this goes."

Logan leaned forward, grabbing two beers out of the mini fridge. He tapped my knee with the amber bottle. Keeping his fingers locked around the neck when I grabbed it, he forced me to meet his gaze. "Do you love her?"

"Love her?" I yanked the bottle from his hand. "I just met her."

"That's not what I asked." Taking a long pull from his beer, he kept his eyes on me. "It's not the worst thing in the world, dude. All I'm saying is you better be sure before you drag her back to Austin and leave her sitting in an apartment while we go out and tear it up on the road. Unless she's down for that. Having a steady piece when we're not touring is cool, as long as she knows the score."

"It's more than that." Reaching in my pocket, I handed him the song I wrote. "I just don't know if I can do it without fucking everything up."

Logan studied the paper, a soft expression that he rarely showed creeping over his face.

"Looks like you already did it. This is some deep shit." He read the lyrics again, looking over at me earnestly. "You won't fuck this up, man."

Nodding, I took a sip of my beer.

Logan leaned forward, clinking his bottle against mine. "To your balls," he chirped. "May they have a long and peaceful life. In Lily's purse or wherever the hell she's keeping them."

I chuckled, suppressing the sly smile that threatened to break out.

"If you knew what that girl did to my balls, you wouldn't be laughing, son. You'd surrender yours in a heartbeat." I raised a brow. "It's that fucking sweet."

Logan roared, his eyes twinkling with mischief. "Do tell."

"Not this time, Logan." Shaking my head, my laugh faded. "Not this time."

The band sat at a long table set up in one of the luxury suites, smiling for the cameras and answering questions for reporters. Christian regaled them with the tale of his adventures at the hospital, while Logan and Sean went on about their love of the Dallas music scene.

When it was my turn, I answered the perfunctory questions about my favorite place to eat in Dallas, the name of my guitar, and my musical influences.

My mouth went dry when a reporter from the Dallas Morning News society column addressed me. "Tell me about your relationship with Lillian Tennison."

My gaze drifted to Lindsey, standing at the back of the room, a ghost of a smile on her lips. What a difference a couple of days made. Lily had gone from a brainless groupie that lacked fashion sense to a commodity she could leverage for publicity.

"No comment."

Lindsey's face fell at my response.

"Is there any truth to the reports that Miss Tennison has moved on to Chad Dyer from Crimson Five? They were spotted dancing together at Rangers in Deep Ellum. And our source confirmed that she is staying at the Omni Hotel."

The reporter looked at me dryly, one hand on her hip, the other holding the mini recorder in front of her. Logan nudged me under the table with his boot.

No comment. No comment. NO COMMENT.

"You need to check your sources." Another nudge from Logan. "Lily is with me."

The reporter perked up. "So I can confirm that you're seeing Lillian Tennison?"

"You can confirm anything you want, lady." Pushing my seat back, I stood. "I don't have any further comments about my girlfriend."

The rest of the guys stood. We followed a girl in a black skirt out the back door to a smaller room.

Logan fell into a chair, grabbing a bottle of water. "Rookie mistake, Cam."

Pacing in a small circle, I shot him a warning glare. "No shit."

This was media 101. Kindergarten stuff. The reporter did a society column, for fuck's sake. It wasn't even a hardball question. Clearly, I wanted to say it. To declare it. I wanted Abigail Tennison to choke on her fucking tea in the morning when she read about me and Lily in the paper.

The door swung open, and Lindsey teetered in on her usual heels, a broad smile plastered on her face.

"Simply wonderful," she cackled. "Normally, I would take your head off for the lack of self-control, Cameron. But Lily Tennison? Your fling is going to make the papers from here to Houston."

"How did a society columnist get access to this press conference, Lindsey?" I stalked toward her. "And how the fuck did she know about Chad?"

Lindsey's eyes were wide as saucers, her usual unflappable demeanor crumbling.

"She called and requested an interview," she said slowly, appraising my reaction to every word. "I didn't see the harm in extending the invitation."

"What about Chad?"

"I might have mentioned—"

"Get out!" Logan roared behind me.

I snapped my head around, wincing at the aftermath. He

was on his feet and at my side in the span of a second.

"Get your shit and get out," he spat. "You're fired."

Lindsey looked helplessly over our shoulders to Christian and Sean. I could see by the expression on her face she wasn't finding any comfort there. Lifting her chin, she squared her shoulders and pulled the bottom of her jacket.

"You don't have to tell me twice," she sputtered. "If I had to spend another day in this godforsaken state, I'd tear my hair out. Good riddance."

Gliding toward the door, she slammed it shut behind her, the thud echoing in the small room.

I looked over my shoulder at Christian and Sean cackling behind me. Throwing an arm around me, Logan tried and failed to keep the amusement out of his voice.

"Like your mama always said, Cam, you can't trust a chick that isn't from Texas."

CHAPTER 22

After the third beer, I relaxed a little. The forty-five minute drive back to Dallas took over three hours with traffic and my little detour to the mall. I turned the small box over in my hand. It was a token. Nothing really. A guitar pick made out of white gold with a tiny diamond on a delicate chain.

Music was my first love, and I would share it with Lily. If I could be as faithful to her as I was to the words I put on paper, we could get through anything.

Jumping out of the limo when it pulled to a stop in front of The Mansion, I turned to Logan when he called my name.

"When you come up for air, we've got a ton of shit to go over," he said, ambling toward me. "Lindsey was a conniving bitch, but we have nobody to handle our tour now. Any suggestions?"

Blowing out a breath, I shrugged. "I'll call Chase. He'll know what to do."

Logan nodded. "The label is gonna shit. They handpicked Lindsey."

"I'm not listening to the label anymore." I placed a hand on his shoulder. "It was stupid to take their advice in the first place. We need to hire local. Someone from Austin. I gotta go."

He smiled. "Get out of here. Go find your balls."

"Right here, buddy." I grabbed my crotch. "Look on the bright side. If I'm off the market, you might actually get some quality pussy."

I made a break for the door before he could chase me. Keeping my head down, I traipsed across the lobby and out the back door. Pulling out my key card, I waited for the green light to push the door open.

"Baby, I'm home," I called. "I hope you're naked."

God, I really hoped she was naked. Or not. Stripping her down was almost as much fun.

Flipping the lights on, I looked around the room. The blanket she was under when I left her was folded neatly. A small twinge worked its way from my chest to my throat.

"Lily?" Pushing the door open to the bedroom, I stood at the threshold.

If I didn't go in, it wouldn't be real. But I knew it was. The room was pristine, the bed made with the coverlet pulled back and two chocolates on the pillow.

Lily's clothes and any trace of her were gone. My shirt, the one she wore to bed, the one I stripped off her every time she did, was folded on the dresser. I walked across the room, flipping on the light in the dark bathroom. Not so much as a strand of her hair remained. Stumbling backward when I realized my knees were actually weak, I felt around for the edge of the bed. I missed it, landing on the floor with a thud.

She'll be back.

I pulled out my phone with shaky hands, dragging my finger across the picture I had taken of her sleeping. Her phone rang once and went to voicemail. I tried again with the same result. Typing out a text, I hit send and stared at the screen.

Please.

If Lily blocked my number, there would be no message that said "delivered" under the text. I waited for five minutes, knowing it took seconds for that little phrase to pop up. It never did.

Dropping my head against the side of the bed, I stared at the ceiling. From the beginning, the thought of hurting Lily had tornented me. The tug I felt in my chest taunted me from the start.

As the pain tore through my gut and the panic settled in my chest, I chuckled. The chuckle turned into a dry laugh when the ceiling went blurry from the moisture that formed in my eyes.

I should've listened to my gut. I was never really afraid of hurting Lily. All along, I was afraid that she would see what I had to offer and it wouldn't be enough. And I guess it wasn't.

I woke up on the sectional in Logan's bungalow. After pillaging the mini bar in my own room, I had stumbled to Logan's in the middle of the night in search of more alcohol. I told him everything. Although how much sense I made was anybody's guess.

I was seated at the table when he emerged from the bedroom. Handing me a bottle of water and three aspirin, he patted me on the shoulder.

"I'm grabbing a shower." He headed for the bedroom. "Limo is picking us up at eleven."

"I'll be there," I mumbled, swallowing the pills and chugging the water.

Pausing at the door, he sighed heavily. "I'm sorry, Cam."

"I'll be fine." Standing, I stretched. "You know what they say: the best way to get over someone is to get under someone else." Waggling my brows, I ambled to the door. "See you at eleven."

The bright sunshine made my eyes water as I trudged toward my bungalow. Pushing open the door, I saw the evidence of last night's debacle strewn about the room. Empty bottles from the mini bar were on the table and the floor. Lily petals from the centerpiece were everywhere.

Shaking my head, I went around the room and collected the bottles, throwing them in the stainless steel trashcan.

I stripped off my clothes and took the fastest shower in history, barely able to stomach standing in the same space where

Lily and I had shared our first shower. And our last.

After packing all my clothes, I rolled the suitcases into the living room and strolled over to the desk to pack my laptop and call for a bellhop.

I sank in the chair when I saw the paper lying on the keyboard. The charcoal drawing of me sleeping that Lily started at her apartment after I spent the night there—she finished it. A message was scrawled in the corner under her signature.

I'm sorry. Please don't hate me.

Dragging my fingers over her name and her farewell, I smudged them into the page until they were barely legible. I dropped the sketch into the wastebasket and watched it drift to the bottom.

After ringing the front desk, I packed up my laptop and hoisted my backpack on my shoulder. I waited by the front door for the bellhop, pulling the door open when he knocked.

"Mr. Knight, I hope you've had a pleasant stay," he said, loading my suitcases onto the cart.

"Fine."

Grabbing my sunglasses from the table, I looked around the room for any items I might have left behind. Only the memory of Lily in every corner of the room and in every object she touched remained. Closing the door, I left it all behind and trudged toward the lobby. The farther I walked, the stronger the ache in my chest became.

I turned and ran for the bungalow. Pushing open the door, I crossed the room and pulled the drawing from the trash.

I'm sorry. Please don't hate me.

Folding the drawing in half, I stowed it in my backpack.

"I've got to make a stop." Sliding into the limo seat, I looked at each of my bandmates.

Logan and Christian nodded while Sean looked out the window. He was the only one that left a girl behind when we started the band. Ally, his high school sweetheart. She was a really nice girl. Sean crawled into a bottle for a month when she married someone else. At the time, I thought it was weak. But if alcohol would make this ache go away, I'd bathe in it.

"Thanks. It won't take too long."

The silence was deafening. Logan scanned the local newspaper, quickly folding it in half and tucking it under his leg. He didn't need to bother. My twitter was blowing up with the news of my "confession." My declaration. My disaster. Downing my vodka and orange juice, I placed the glass in the cup holder, wiping my sweaty palm on my jeans when we pulled to a stop.

"I'll be right back." Swinging the door wide, I stepped out, searching for any landmarks to jar my memory.

I headed up the cement path, hooking a left at the first set of doors. Ducking into the alcove, I spotted the familiar mat in front of the door to Lily's apartment.

I kneeled down and lifted the mat, pulling the small plastic bag that contained the necklace with the gold pick out of my pocket. Laying it next to the solitary key, I replaced the mat and pushed to my feet. I pressed my forehead to the door, cursing her under my breath even as I said a silent prayer for her to find me there. It took a good five minutes to tear myself away. Turning, I ignored the tug in my chest and walked back along the same path I had come on.

CHAPTER 23

"We love you, Dallas! Goodnight!" Logan shouted into the mic as the audience went wild.

Pulling the strap off my neck, I handed the guitar to one of our roadies and headed toward the light at the side of the stage. The crew for the next band brushed past me in a frenzy to set up their equipment while ours was being torn down.

My t-shirt clung to my damp skin, chilling me in the night air as I pushed through the curtain. The crowd was whipped into a frenzy after our last number. The air was electric with excitement, and the ground shook beneath us.

"Fuck yeah!" Logan turned, pulling me in for a bear hug. "You were on fire!" He pulled back, taking my head between his hands.

"Fuck yeah, I was!" I yelled above the roar.

"That was amazing!" Sean crashed into my back, throwing an arm around my neck.

I turned and gave him a hearty pat on the back. The high of performing had me on top of a mountain. My head was in the clouds as we pushed our way to the dressing room. Christian ambled behind us, talking to one of the crew.

Grabbing a beer from the bucket filled with ice in the hallway, I twisted the cap and downed half in one gulp.

"Lookie-lookie." Logan whistled, turning to me and raising a brow. Twenty or so girls lined the hallway in front of our dressing room. Blonds, brunettes, and redheads. It was a smorgasbord of perfect tits and firm asses in tight micro minis.

"Betty or Veronica?" he yelled over his shoulder at me as he waded into the adoring crowd.

Downing the last half of my beer, I slid between two girls, pulling them to my sides. They squealed their approval, running their hands over my chest, my stomach, and my ass.

Arching a brow at Logan, I slid my hand to Blondie's ass and squeezed.

"Both."

My head was pounding.

Pounding. Pounding.

Jerking up, I looked around the dark room. I ran my hand over my bare chest, my eyes adjusting to the single beam of light that cut through the blackout curtains.

Pounding. Pounding.

"Open the fucking door!" Logan's voice and more pounding.

Shit. Sliding off the bed, I wobbled to my feet.

"I'm coming!" I stumbled toward the door. "Stop the fucking —" pulling the door open, I reeled back like a vampire against the harsh light in the hallway, "—pounding," I groaned.

"It's about fucking time. I've been out there for ten minutes." Logan brushed past me, stalking to the window and throwing open the drapes. "Our plane leaves in two hours."

"Oh, God," I groaned, walking listlessly to the bed and falling on top of it. "I'm dying."

He chuckled. "You're not dying, you fucking pussy."

I *was* dying. Or I was dead.

"What the fuck happened?" I buried my face in the pillow.

The very cool, soft pillow. It was the best fucking pillow I'd ever felt.

"To you?" Logan smiled, dropping onto the couch and planting his feet on the coffee table. "About a fifth of Jack."

Lifting my head, I looked around. "Where is everyone?"

Bits and pieces of the night filtered through my foggy brain. Betty and Veronica. The limo. I tried to piece it together.

"Sean and Christian are downstairs." Logan stifled a yawn.

"What about...the girls?" I swallowed hard.

The girl. My girl. *Lily.* If I was going to have a bout of amnesia, why couldn't it be her that was erased from my memory? I rubbed my bare chest, the ache returning the moment I thought of her.

"What girls?" He snorted. "The ones you chased off with your whining about Lily? Her hair, her eyes, her feet...really, bro? Her feet?"

"She has cute toes," I blurted. "So I didn't—"

"Nail Betty and Veronica? Fuck, dude, you couldn't." He smirked. "After you drank all the Jack, you curled in a ball and passed out."

Great. Lily not only ripped my heart out, she took my balls along for the ride.

"I'm going to grab some breakfast." Logan pushed to his feet. "Take a shower. You stink."

I pulled the pillow over my head.

"We're leaving in thirty minutes." Stalking over to me, he kicked my leg. "With or without you."

"I'll be there," I grumbled.

I wanted to get out of Dallas as fast as I could. Two hundred miles away from Lily might be far enough to cure the ache.

My stomach dropped as the elevator descended. I pressed my back against the wall when we stopped at different floors and more people piled in. By the time we got to the lobby, I could feel the bile rising in my throat.

Pulling my sunglasses from the neck of my t-shirt, I slipped them on, ignoring the remaining Jack that sloshed around in my empty stomach. The whoosh of cool air hit my face when the doors slid open. Hoisting my backpack higher on my shoulder, I took a few steps into the atrium and knelt down to tie my shoe.

A pair of high heels stepped into my line of sight, stopping just short of the tips of my boots. I looked up, my gaze falling on the white gold pick hanging from the delicate chain and then up to the sky blue eyes. My hand was frozen, my fingers wrapped in the laces of my boots.

The crease on Lily's forehead deepened the longer I stared.

"C-Cameron." She took a deep breath. "I'm sorry."

Pushing to my feet, I looked down at her hesitantly. "Lily, what are you doing here?"

"I came to apologize. I didn't know what to do." Looking down, her hand went to her neck, fidgeting with the pendant. "I got scared."

The urge to grab her and wrap her in my arms was so strong my fingers curled into fists at my side. "Scared of me—of us?"

"N-no." Blinking up at me, tears welled in her eyes. "Of everything."

Softening, I ran my hand down her arm, lacing our fingers. "Baby, what are you scared of?"

"A lot of things." She gave me a watery smile. "I talked to my father. He just wants me to be happy. And I can't be happy without you. I-I want us to be together. But I don't even know what that looks like."

"Like this." Slipping my hand in her hair, I cupped her neck, tilting her face to gently brush a kiss to her lips. She stood, fixed in her spot. Breathing with me. Being with me. Her eyes locked with mine.

"And like this." I kissed her again. Falling into her. She parted her lips, a deep sigh escaping a second before her tongue tangled with mine slowly. So slowly.

Bending time in that way that she did, the last twenty-four

hours disappeared along with the ache in my chest.

CHAPTER 24

TWO MONTHS LATER

"I t's a full house." Logan burst in the room, clapping his hands and rubbing them together feverishly. "You know who's out there?"

Glancing at him, I continued to jot down the lyrics that were filling my head. I wrote like a demon when Lily and I were apart. I managed to convince the guys to stay in Austin for the last couple of months while we worked on songs for the next album. Yeah, I had my reasons. And they knew it.

It turned out for the best. Every time I returned from my weekly trip to Dallas, I had a new song to work on for our weekend shows at The Parish. Caged was playing a prolonged engagement at my brother's club. It wasn't a hardship. The Parish was the largest venue in Austin, and the biggest bands in the country graced the stage from time to time.

"Dylan Boothe *and* Liam McConnell," Logan whooped. "FRONT ROW."

Sean crashed through the door with Christian hot on his heels. "Guess who's here?"

"Dylan and Liam," I deadpanned, trying to hide my smile when his face fell.

Dylan Boothe and Liam McConnell were the lead singers for Leveraged and Revenged Theory, respectively. Along with Drafthouse, they made up the "Big Three:" the powerhouse trio of bands that hailed from Austin. They dominated the charts and sold out venues from coast to coast.

"What do you think they're doing here?" Sean grabbed a beer from the bucket on the table and twisted off the cap. "And where's the rest of the crew?"

We knew every member of the Big Three, but not well.

I shrugged. "They're not touring right now." Chewing on the pen I was holding, I reclined against the cushions of the couch. "I heard Leveraged is cutting an album in L.A."

"I'm surprised Tori let them stray that far from home base," Logan said, motioning for me to throw him a beer. "She keeps pretty close tabs on them. I don't know how they can stand it, letting their manager call all the shots."

I raised a brow at Logan.

"I know, I know." He rolled his eyes. "She's not a 'regular' manager, but she's not performing anymore. I had to do a double-take when I saw her in the paper a couple weeks ago. She was wearing a suit. I mean, it was a chick suit, and she looked pretty fucking fine, but it was still a suit."

"Dude." Christian shook his head incredulously. "You know why she doesn't perform. Have a little empathy."

Logan looked down at his boots. The room fell silent for a moment, the way it always did when someone spoke about Tori Grayson. She was our age, no more than twenty-six, but she was a legend. Her band, Damaged, was the first band out of Austin in two decades to hit it big. Huge. Tragically, they were cut down at the height of their fame. A freak bus accident took Rhenn Grayson, Tori's husband and the genius front man for Damaged, and Paige Dawson, her best friend and their lead guitarist.

"Who cares how she looks—it's a miracle she's still breathing," Christian said quietly. "She broke nearly every bone in her body." Wincing, he reached reflexively for his ribs. The injury was slow to heal, taking a month before he was able to walk around without taping his ribs. And he was only in the hospital overnight. Tori had been in a rehab center for months.

Looking at the clock above the door, I felt the band around my chest tighten. Lily was on the road, making the two hundred mile trip from Dallas. The thought of her bleeding or broken from an accident turned my blood to ice water. The girl was still too stubborn for her own good. She wouldn't let me buy her a car. At least she agreed to "borrow" mine. I promptly went out and bought a Mercedes SUV, the safest one on the market.

"Where's Lily?" Logan read my expression, his brow furrowing.

"She's on her way." I glanced at the clock again.

Sean stood up to grab a beer, nodding toward my phone. "Call her."

The guys loved Lily. They prodded her almost as much as I did about making the move to Austin. I almost cracked Sean in the head one day when I heard him talking to her about handcuffs, until I realized he was threatening to kidnap her and bring her here by force.

My leg bobbed as I waited for her to answer. "Hey, baby!" I barely heard Lily's voice over the blast of music in the background. It was so loud, I nearly burst an eardrum. "Turn the music down!"

I released the shout a second after the music died in the background.

"What are you yelling at, Cam?" she said, the amusement in her voice evident.

The guys sipped their beer, taking in the floorshow. Since girls weren't allowed in the dressing room any longer, this was the only entertainment they got anymore.

"Nothing." Raising my brows at them, I put my index finger to my lips. "Where are you?"

She let out a sigh. "We go through this every time. If I tell you where I'm at, you're going to start worrying. If I hit traffic, you'll be distracted when you go onstage. I'll be there in a little while."

"Ok." Chewing my lip, I raked a hand through my hair. "Be careful."

"I will. I love you."

It never got old. Not the first time she said it, the night she found me in the lobby of the Omni, and not now.

"I love you too, baby. So damn much."

"I love you, Lily. So much," Logan mimicked me in a high-pitched voice, making smacking noises as he leaned toward the phone. He jumped back when I jerked the beer bottle I was holding, spewing suds on his vintage Pearl Jam t-shirt.

"Asshole," he muttered.

Lily cracked up. "Be nice. I'll see you soon."

Clicking the button on the side of the phone when it went dark, I looked down at her picture. The only thing worse than not having her here was having her here part-time. I glanced at clocks and counted minutes, whether she was here or there, only getting any peace when we were so close I could feel her breath.

Three loud raps on the door brought me to the present. Moving to the door, Logan looked over his shoulder at me. I raised a brow in warning.

"I know, you big pussy," he groused, leveling me with a glare as he pulled the door open. "No chicks in the dressing room."

"Well, I'm in the clear," Dylan Boothe said as he sauntered in, an easy smile on his face, "since I don't have a vagina." He turned and looked at Liam who was a step behind. "Better wait outside, Liam."

The room burst into a fit of cackles.

"Very funny, asshat." Liam chuckled.

Sean reached into the metal ice bucket, offering the guys a beer.

They took it gratefully, surveying the dressing room.

Dylan leaned against the wall. "Sweet setup you guys got here. I wouldn't mind spending a few weeks at home."

"I wouldn't mind selling out a few of those arenas." Logan chuckled. "But we needed a break. Why are you guys in town?"

"Eh, Tori called a meeting." Dylan shrugged, letting his eyes drift around the dressing room. "She's announcing a big memorial concert at Zilker for Rhenn and Paige."

The event would be major if it was taking place at Zilker. The Big Three were the only acts large enough to bring in the kind of crowd it would take to fill it. The fact that it was a memorial show for the greatest band that ever came from these parts only sweetened the pot.

"That sounds epic." Taking a sip of my beer, I glanced at the clock. Again.

"Are y'all touring soon?" Dylan looked confused when my band mates turned to me.

"What are y'all looking at me for?" I raised a brow. "I'm not the one that books the tours. And I didn't fire our manager."

"Hey!" Logan protested. "I was standing up for your girl, man. Remember?"

Nodding, I smiled.

"You know, I could talk to Taryn for you," Dylan offered. "She might be able to solve your management issue. No promises though."

"Taryn?" Crossing his arms, Logan waited for Dylan to elaborate. "I thought y'all were exclusive with Tori?"

Dylan took a sip of his beer. "Taryn is Tori's partner. Well, kind of. She managed Damaged when Tori was still playing in the band. Everyone always gives Tori credit, because of the story, you know?" His smile faded a little. The story. The tragedy. "And she's always managed Leveraged. She's Derik's girl. *Was* Derik's girl," he amended.

I didn't have a nemesis, but if I did, it would be Derik, the guitarist for Leveraged. He did most of the writing and arranging, the same way I did for Caged. And the boy could shred a guitar.

"Where is Derik?" I was going for casual, but I didn't fail to notice Logan's smirk.

"Working out some shit in L.A." Dylan shifted his gaze to Liam. A tense look passed between them. "He'll be home soon. He's seeing someone out there. But she ain't from Texas."

Liam snorted. "And she ain't Taryn."

"Anyway." Dropping his bottle in the big, metal trashcan, Dylan turned to Logan. "I'll talk to Taryn about y'all after the concert. She's got a lot on her plate right now. Are you guys in a big rush? Signing with her is worth the wait."

We all nodded when Dylan's gaze swept the room. Signing with Twin Souls, Tori's management company, would definitely be worth the wait. But I wasn't holding my breath. We weren't signing with some junior manager, even if it was at the most sought after management company in the country. Tori was notorious for turning down any band that directly competed with the Big Three. Not that we were in the same league, but we were close. We were all from Austin and played similar music.

"Thanks, man." Logan patted Dylan on the back. "We'd really appreciate it."

"No problem." He motioned at Liam, who pushed to his feet. "We'll let y'all get ready. Think of this as an audition." He pulled open the door. "I might record a little something- something to show Taryn."

Lifting my chin to them, I smiled nervously. The other guys did the same.

Logan's laugh died the minute he closed the door behind Dylan and Liam.

"We can't suck." Logan leaned against the wall, his face losing a little color. "We absolutely can't suck," he repeated, taking a long pull from his beer.

The door creaked open, and my heart jumped into my throat.

"You never suck, Logan," Lily said, patting him on the arm as she walked toward me.

All the tension left my body when I heard her voice. Time slowed down, and everything inside me stilled when she leaned over to kiss me.

"Hey, you," I breathed, easing her onto my lap.

"That's our cue," Christian said, smiling at us as the guys headed for the door.

"See you after the show, Lil," Sean said, following Christian into the hall.

"No screwing on the couch. We all have to use it." Logan snorted, pulling the door closed behind him.

It popped open a second later, and Logan peeked his head inside.

"Glad you're here, darlin'."

"Me, too." Lily smiled at him warmly.

The door barely clicked shut before I had her back against the couch and my mouth on hers. She tugged at my hair, pulling me back.

"What's your hurry?" she cooed, pulling me in for a slow kiss.

It was probably then, when she stilled my heart with that phrase the first time we were together, that I fell in love with her.

"No hurry, baby." I pressed my forehead to hers. "Although, I was hoping for a little action before the show."

Grinding my hips against hers, I slid my tongue along her bottom lip.

"Later." She pushed my chest with her small fists. "You've got a show to do, and I've got to unpack."

I liked the sound of that. It meant she would be here more than a day before she disappeared, leaving only her scent in my bed and her little love notes scattered around my apartment.

Pushing off the couch, I walked over to the mirror, raking my hands through my hair. She met my gaze in the reflection, a smile tilting up the corners of her lips.

"Don't look at me like that," I warned. "I'll make all those people out there wait and throw you up against the wall."

Keeping her eyes locked on mine, she stood and walked over, pressing her chest to my back. Her hands skimmed my chest.

"I hope you still feel like that when the novelty wears off and I'm around all the time," She murmured.

I could impress her and tell her that it would be thirty-three days until she was here for good—792 hours. I couldn't give her the exact minutes. Right now. Sometimes I figured it out in my head, on days when I really missed her. But right now she was pressed against me, and my mind was quiet.

Turning, I cupped her cheek. "I can't wait until you're here to stay, baby. It's killing me."

Wrapping her arms around my neck, she looked up at me.

"Me, too. That's why I finished my last project early. I'm officially a graduate." She rose up to her tiptoes, her lips hovering an inch from mine. "I hope you were serious about wanting a roommate. Since everything I own is packed in your car."

I searched her face. No telltale crease on her forehead. No hesitation. My shock gave way to relief. And then want. As strong as the pull in my chest that bound us.

"You're serious?" I pressed a kiss to her bottom lip.

She nodded, her smile brilliant. "I couldn't keep leaving or watching you go. I love you too much."

Before she could say another word, my mouth was on hers, swallowing her giggles and the moans that followed.

The cheers from the audience began to shake the walls. It was my cue. The opening act was finished. It was time for the main event.

THE END

ACKNOWLEDGEMENTS

Matthew—The first person I ever loved more than myself.

Victoria—The younger, better versions of me that makes my life worth living.

Dennis and Charlotte—I love you both. Don't be so surprised.

Mary—Love you. Enough said.

Bonnie Marie—Forever wild. I miss you.

Dina—My sister soulmate.

And finally, gratefully, Ally Bishop. You see the story and help me make it better.

Jayne Frost, Author

So…Who is Jayne?

As a writer you would think that would be a simple question…but it's not. I spend so much time living in my characters heads, listening to their voices, that sometimes I forget about my own.

I guess I should start with the basics. The backstory. I was born and raised in California. At this point I'm usually asked what it was like to grow up near the beach, but sadly, I don't know. I grew up in the "other" part of California. Perfect for an aspiring writer, if you ask me. You learn a lot about keeping yourself busy when the nearest house is a mile away…and it belongs to your grandparents.

I spent all my time with my nose in a book, living vicariously through the characters, until I wrote a book of my own. I was 10 at the time. It was a scintillating piece that cast the family pet as the protagonist.

By the time I went to high school, I moved on to romance.

Why? Because I met my very own prince charming. I wrote love poems in my journal about the green eyed boy that stole my heart. He promised, the way all storybook hero's do, to sweep me away and take me on a grand adventure. And he did.

We picked up and moved to the Lone Star State, and began the story of us. The best stories begin without a road map or a compass. Veering off course makes the journey so much more interesting.

True to form, just when I thought my life was set, we started the next adventure. I traded in my cowboy boots and followed my green eyed boy to Las Vegas. My home will always be in Texas, but my heart is anywhere that he is. Our beautiful daughter made the journey with us. Our son stayed in Texas, to write his own story.

Somehow, in the midst of the chaos that is our life, I find time to write. Writing is what I love. I might stray from the romance every now and then if that is what moves me…but I always come back. Some of the stories don't seem romantic at all. They are gritty stories about flawed characters that find each other and hold on tight. Those are the stories that speak to me. Because that's life. I believe that every story should have a happy ending- even the difficult ones.

Find me at www.jaynefrost.com, on Twitter (@jaynefrostbooks), and Facebook (Jayne Frost), and feel free to email me via my website (look for the "Contact" tab!)

Thank you so much for reading *Gone for You!* If you have a moment, please leave a review on your favorite book websites.

Made in the USA
Middletown, DE
08 July 2019